DEADLY DOUBLE-CROSS

When Carlos Williams is asked to lead a rescue mission, it's to find and rescue the kidnapped wife and children of a local rancher. The risk is that their captors, a band of Comancheros, will sell them in Mexico City, into a life of slavery or worse. Little knowing the tragedies he faces, Carlos is determined to find his charges — whatever it takes. And, as it turns out, this mission is going to take everything he has . . .

KEVIN McCARTHY

DEADLY DOUBLE-CROSS

Complete and Unabridged

LINFORD
Leicester

First published in Great Britain in 2011 by
Robert Hale Limited
London

First Linford Edition
published 2012
by arrangement with
Robert Hale Limited
London

British Library CIP Data

McCarthy, Kevin.
  Deadly double-cross. - -
  (Linford western library)
  1. Western stories.
  2. Large type books.
  I. Title II. Series
  823.9′2–dc23

  ISBN 978–1–4448–1094–3

Published by
F. A. Thorpe (Publishing)
Anstey, Leicestershire

Set by Words & Graphics Ltd.
Anstey, Leicestershire
Printed and bound in Great Britain by
T. J. International Ltd., Padstow, Cornwall

This book is printed on acid-free paper

1

Carlos Williams stepped out of the Big Springs Bank, into the boiling heat of the mid-July Texan sun. At 9.30 in the morning it was already hot enough to fry an egg on Main Street.

With all his business transactions completed and the money he'd been paid by the army for mustangs he'd caught and broken safely deposited, there was nothing left for him to do but climb into the saddle and head off home.

He gently kneed his elegant pinto forward, the lead-ropes of his two rangy packhorses gripped firmly in his left hand; he happily anticipated the look of pleasure that would soon be on Nadie's face when he gave her that new dress he'd bought for her coming birthday.

It had taken some doing, getting her size and all; picking out the dress from the Montgomery Ward catalogue without her knowing what he and Nora Harding, owner of the general store, and co-conspirator, had been up to. But Nora had managed it somehow without Nadie becoming suspicious, and the order had been sent, along with twenty dollars, all the way to Chicago.

After several months of anxious waiting the dress had arrived, and in time for Nadie's birthday next week. It was, at this very moment, carefully wrapped in fancy pink paper and tied with a big yellow bow, and packed with great care into the pinto's saddle-bags. Not by Carlos but by Nora.

'You just can't stuff it in there like that, Carlos, it'll crease up,' she'd scolded, taking the dainty parcel from him and carefully placing it in the saddle-bags herself.

Passing the blacksmith's, Carlos wasn't surprised to see that it was closed for the day. The owner, Harvey Boscombe had probably tied one on last night in the saloon, and didn't feel like opening up today.

With their relationship being never friendly anyway, Carlos felt little sympathy for the blacksmith.

He was just drawing opposite the jailhouse when the door opened and Henry Dodds, sheriff of Big Springs, stepped out into the street, calling a greeting to him, 'Morning, Carlos. Heading home?'

'Yeah, Henry. Fort Bravos was happy to get those ponies, but not as happy as I'll be to get home to Nadie. Two months on the trail is a long time.'

'Yep, I reckon a man loses sight of time on a long trail drive, but it makes it a damn sight more comforting knowing he has a pretty wife waiting back home for him.'

'You sure got that right, Henry.'

'Carlos, I know you're itchin' to get home, but there's been some trouble at the Englishman, Clarence Dunsford's spread. Indian trouble maybe. Anyway, could you stop off there on your way and take a looksee. Jeb Claiborne asked if you'd call in; he rode out there about two hours ago. I'd go myself but this damn hip is playing up again.'

Some years back, Henry Dodds had got in the way of a band of Comanches coming back from a raid into Mexico. He'd put up a stiff fight, though he had been badly wounded by a stone-tipped arrow through his thigh. True to their code, the Comanches, honouring his bravery, had called off the attack after he had killed seven of them. They had saluted him by raising their lances high and had then ridden away, leaving Henry to live or die out there in the badlands of Texas.

Henry had proved to be a fighter in more ways than one; against all odds he lived but he walked with a bad limp from then on.

'Sure, Henry, it's not all that far out of my way.'

'Thanks, son, I knew I could count on you.'

Several hours later Carlos rode into Dunsford's front yard, where a crowd of men were gathered.

'Here's the Injun now, Mr Dunsford.'

'The 'breed'll catch 'em soon enough.'

'Hell, everyone knows it takes an Injun ter catch an Injun.' This last statement came from Harvey Boscombe.

So here he is, thought Carlos; wherever trouble was brewing there was Harvey.

Applying a tight rein and keeping the pinto's head high, he moved the horse forward, not allowing him to dodge around any of the men and forcing them to move aside or have the pony knock them down.

They knew he did that on purpose, showing his contempt for them; they didn't like it but they moved. They also saw that Carlos kept his right hand close to the Colt at his side, and most knew the skills with a pistol this man on the pinto pony possessed.

Carlos knew Clarence Dunsford only by sight, having never had any reason to talk to him before, even though the two were neighbours. Dunsford moved in different circles from Carlos.

He stopped the pinto where Dunsford

stood and the man, obviously agitated, reached out suddenly, roughly grabbing the bridle of the astonished horse.

'Can you tell who did this?' He pointed at his yard.

The pinto tried to dance away, fiddle-prancing from foot to foot, not being used to such treatment and not liking it.

The question was abrupt, without preamble; the mark of a man obviously used to getting his own way. Carlos looked about, taking his time, making sure to let Dunsford know that he too, was his own man.

The big, double-storeyed house Dunsford had built of sawn timber and stone was now nothing more than a smouldering heap of ashes, likewise the barn and bunkhouse.

The male household staff, all Mexican, were scattered about the yard, pin-cushioned by dozens of arrows. All had been decapitated and now their heads adorned various poles and rails about the corral.

They seemed to have put up a bit of a fight with what weapons they had to hand, pitchforks, scythes and clubs, but their pitiful weapons had been no match against arrows and rifles.

The older women had been stripped naked, raped, then butchered with tomahawks. The younger ones would have been carried off as future slaves, to be sold to wealthy Spaniards or Mexicans in Mexico City.

Carlos examined an arrow Dunsford handed up to him, noticing the markings and the way the feathers were fletched to the shaft. They were Kwahadi clan Comanche, Quanah Parker's tribe.

These were renegades who refused to change their warlike way of life, preferring to continue raiding and making war on Mexicans, Apaches and whites alike.

The depredations upon the ranch and the mutilating of the Dunsford staff were clear examples of their savagery and hatred for all things that were not Comanche.

He also saw the deep indented ruts

made by the big, heavy, two-wheeled *carretas*, the typical Mexican ox-carts, made of riverbank cottonwood. Strong and sturdily built, they were used to carry the renegades' supplies.

He'd seen these wagons before: being this far from Mexico, they were usually used only by a certain brand of men.

'Well?'

He waited a few seconds before he spoke. 'Comancheros, with some renegade Kwahadi Comanche.'

'Good God!' It was obvious by the sudden horror on his face at the mention of the name Comanchero that Dunsford too, had heard of them, and that the news shook him to the core. 'How long ago?'

Carlos shrugged. 'A day, maybe, no more.'

'Where are they headed?'

Carlos was thoughtful. 'Probably Mexico City. They'll sell whatever captives they've taken on their trading trip with the Comanches there.'

Dunsford stiffened at those words; a

worried frown crossed his face. 'Can we catch them before they get to the border?'

He sure was a man with a burr under his saddle, itching for revenge, but then who could blame him? He'd just had all his help killed and his spread destroyed, burned to the ground.

'Maybe! There are about forty or so of them and they have many captives and considerable plunder from trading with the Comanches. But they have to follow the waterholes at this time of the year, so they have to travel slowly. The Rio Grande's about a hundred miles away, so it will take them about a week to get there. They'll probably do twenty miles a day, maybe a bit less. If they travel too fast they'll kill some of the captives and there's no profit in a dead body.'

'So you're saying they could be apprehended?'

'A small party, say ten or twelve men travelling light, could maybe catch them before they get to the border.'

'Good, excellent. When can we get started?' demanded Dunsford.

It riled Williams to think the rancher would just naturally assume that he would help. He looked at the men gathered there, and knew they were watching, waiting for his reply.

He had known and worked with nearly all of them on and off over the years. He knew that several of them looked upon him with contempt as an Apache half-breed. Son of a squaw-man. Harvey Boscombe just plain hated him.

Some of the others considered him more white than Indian but none of them had ever invited him into their homes or to the saloon to drink with them after a cattle drive, or a hard week's branding.

Carlos felt he owed them nothing.

Clarence Dunsford was an Englishman, a man with funny ways some said and an even funnier way of talking, but he was rich so he was accepted.

He had bought his ranch, after coming west from Boston three years ago, calling it The Strand, for reasons known only to himself. He was making a good living raising Hereford beef, strange-looking cattle he had brought with him from England.

He had experimentally crossed these animals with Texas longhorns and the results were surprising; the animals quickly put on extra meat and he was able to gain a contract to supply the army with beef. Occasionally he would drive some of them up north for shipment to the the beef-hungry markets in the East.

Carlos, while understanding how the Englishman must be feeling, acknowledged to himself that he didn't know Dunsford all that well, certainly not well enough to go charging off tracking men who would just as soon kill you as spit. Besides, he had visions of Nadie in her new dress and just how pleased she was going to be.

'Now hang on a minute,' he said, looking Dunsford straight in the eye. 'I've just taken a string of mustangs to Fort Bravos in New Mexico and I've been away for two months. I'm tired and all I want to do is get back to my own spread. I'm sorry for your loss, Mr Dunsford, but this is Texas; you can build again like many of us here have had to do in the past.'

There were angry mutterings from the men gathered there in the yard that was still reeking of blood and death and smoke.

'I'll give you three times as much as you've made from selling those horses.'

'It's not the money. It's time I went home.'

Just then Jeb Claiborne stepped up and placed his hand gently on the saddle, 'Carlos, they took Mr Dunsford's wife and two young daughters. If they're allowed to get away with this then none of us will ever be safe from their raids. I understand that you want to get back home, but you're the best damned tracker in Texas. If I weren't so danged old I'd be going myself, but if you oblige Mr Dunsford I'll throw in that big black you broke in for me last July on top of what Mr Dunsford's offered to pay you. That'd be my contribution.'

Dunsford hadn't mentioned his women-folk being taken, so that of course changed everything. A man in these parts had to stand up and be counted when something like this happened to a neighbour. And Carlos was no exception. He'd already said what he felt about the money, but the offer of that horse, well, Carlos just couldn't let that go.

He'd be perfect for breeding his own string of quality horseflesh, and that stallion sure was some horse. Mean, suspicious and just downright ornery.

Carlos and that horse had a lot in common.

However, it was Harvey Boscombe who finally sealed the deal as far as Carlos was concerned.

'Hell, everyone knows an Apache's a damn sight better at stealing than farming, and Carlos ain't no different just cause he's got some white blood in him. Maybe he just wants to hurry home to his woman.' A dirty, suggestive laugh left his lips. 'Hell who wouldn't? I know I would. So let's just form a posse and make the damned breed here guide us, at gunpoint if we have to.'

Something went off inside Carlos.

Without warning he heeled the pinto quickly to where Harvey sat his own horse. Before the big blacksmith knew what was happening Carlos had pulled his Colt and smacked the long, heavy barrel smartly on top of the startled man's head.

Boscombe's eyes crossed, he let out a soft whimper and toppled sideways off his horse.

There was again angry muttering among some of the men, especially those who were friends of Harvey's, men like Fes Bishop and Clem Abbots but the gun was still held in Carlos's unwavering hand, so no one started anything.

Jeb Claiborne spoke up then, his thin reedy voice silencing them, cutting through the afternoon heat. He was at least seventy years old but he too was a rich man. He had been one of the first Texas settlers and other men listened to him. 'Now Harvey had that coming, boys, and no mistake. There's no need for such talk. If Carlos here rides for Mr Dunsford it will be because he accepts the offers made, not because he's bulldogged into it.'

There was rising anger in Carlos now and when he spoke they could plainly hear it in his voice 'I'll track for you, Mr Dunsford; but you and at least a dozen other men need to be ready to leave in a couple of hours. Mr Claiborne, that big black will do just fine.'

His tone was hard, with an edge, as he looked at the scowling men helping Harvey Boscombe to stand on shaking legs, blood running down his face.

'You won't forget to give me a bill of sale for him, Mr Claiborne? I'd hate to be accused of horse stealing.'

He turned the pinto and rode off home to gather up his war bag and tell Nadie why he'd be gone for the next few weeks.

At first she was disappointed, but being an Apache she was also a fatalist, taking life as it came and not fighting against what she could not control. She knew also that she too could be on her way right now to Mexico City, as a slave.

However, she was thoughtful as she helped him pack the things he'd need. 'I do not trust some of these men you will lead against the Comanchero and Comanche scum. That blacksmith is as deceitful as any Comanche.'

'Don't worry. Most of them are good men at heart,' he reassured her brightly, though in his own heart he knew she was right. 'The others . . . ' he shrugged, and then held her tightly. 'Well, they will have a fight on their hands if they decide to do away with me.' He kissed her playfully and moved away.

He took down several boxes of ammunition from a cupboard, went to the corner of the study and picked up his Apache war bow and quiver, full of arrows. In the hands of an Indian, a well placed arrow would kill as easily as a bullet and was less noisy.

At last he was ready. He left the house to saddle another horse, giving the pinto a well needed rest. He loaded up the saddle-bags with the supplies he would need on the trail. He slung the bow and quiver across his back, then turned to Nadie.

He kissed her gently. 'Save that dress for when I get back. I might even take you into town, where you can just put those other women to shame.' He mounted quickly, waved goodbye and trotted out of the yard.

He could hear cattle bawling as Nadie's brother, Nairn, worked the herd over to the southern boundary, taking them to the good grass fed by the river that meandered through the centre of his spread, making it such a prize in this harsh, dry corner of south-west Texas.

2

The black horse remembered him and nudged him with its velvety nose. He had no problems putting his saddle on the strong, broad back.

'He's a fine horse, I'm kinda sorry to lose him.' Jeb Claiborne ran his hand down the sleek, glossy neck of the big horse. The stallion was eager to go and pranced away, rearing like a young colt. Carlos gently fought him down.

'Why'd you offer him, Jeb? You're not obligated to Clarence Dunsford.'

'No, son, I ain't but I'd like to see the man get his family back. I'm certain sure that if anybody can get them back for him it's you, but I think you're gonna need all the aces you can get to do it. I just gave you one; the rest you'll have to deal for yourself.'

'You're a good man, Jeb.'

Claiborne looked up, squinting into

the sun. 'Times are changing here in Texas, Carlos. The day is coming when men won't be able to just take what they want. Law and order, courts, schools for the kids, the railroad. It'll all happen one day. Now don't lose that deed to the horse; and son, you better keep a look out for Harvey Boscombe and his friends; the Comancheros may just be the least of your worries.'

On the ride back to Dunsford's spread, Carlos let the big black horse get a bit of that pent up energy out of his system. Then, when he settled into a ground-eating canter, his rider began to relax.

It didn't last long, for soon he could see the milling crowd of men, some standing holding reins in their hands, others already mounted, all waiting for him.

Dunsford was all set, waiting impatiently to be off. The men who had volunteered to go were mostly good men with guns and horses and would be handy when the time came to fight, which it surely would.

Carlos was surprised to see Harvey Boscombe among the men, but was gratified that Boscombe was wearing a bandage on his head. Dunsford must have offered them plenty for Harvey to bring his aching head along. He looked at Carlos with hate filled eyes but held his silence.

In the late-afternoon light Carlos began to cast around the yard looking for sign.

A sizeable army had come upon the house, consisting of the Mexican traders known as Comancheros. For many years these men travelled to and fro through Comancheria, the name given to the lands held by the savage, war-loving Comanche. The Comanche killed all white men found by them and took their womenfolk captive to be used as trade goods with the Comancheros, a profitable business, so therefore the Mexican traders travelled with impunity throughout Comanche territory in the name of trade.

Maybe forty of this particular band were made up of fighting men: Comancheros and Comanche braves; the rest were the captive slaves to be sold. These would more than likely be white women and perhaps even some Apache squaws taken in previous Comanche raids.

The Apaches and Comanches hated each other about as much as they hated the white men, but it never stopped either side from stealing each others' people if the chance occurred; selling them as slaves or raising them as their own.

A sudden thought struck Carlos as he studied the sign.

The Comanche usually protected the Comancheros and gave them safe passage in and out of their land. If, however, alcohol had been traded, and that was probably a sure bet, then the Indians, once drunk on that firewater, were known to become extremely unpredictable.

The Comancheros usually buried whatever gutrot they had brought with them to trade, about a full day's ride from the Comanche village, simply as a safety precaution.

When the trading was finished, the Comancheros would quickly start for home — even they could only take so much of the devil's hospitality — but they would always leave a hostage behind who would, usually, half a day after his companions had left, lead the Indians to the buried alcohol. Before they had a chance to get drunk, the hostage was already high-tailing it after his outfit. Comanches were fire-breathing demons straight from hell when they were sober; drunk — well that was something else again.

This is what Carlos looked for now. He could not see where a single rider had as yet come following hard after the main band.

If no rider had come, then maybe he was still on the way and would arrive here sooner or later.

It would be dark in about twenty minutes, so Carlos went to find Clarence Dunsford.

'So you think one of them will make an appearance here soon?'

'Nothing is certain, but it's a good guess. They usually trade alcohol, no reason to think they haven't this time.'

'But this waiting will surely put them even further ahead of us?'

Carlos could see the fear and worry in the other man's face. No man should ever have to face such horror.

'The Comancheros and — Comanches too — have enemies; they must pass through the land of the Apache before they get to the border. The Apache and the Mexicans are mortal enemies. These bandits cannot afford to rush; if they press their animals too hard they'll kill them. They don't want to be on foot in Apache territory. We'll catch them up.'

The distant drumming of horses hoofs silenced any further discussion. 'Looks like you were right,' Dunsford said, gazing with a new found respect at the younger man, then he turned away to the others. 'Quickly, hide yourselves,' he whispered.

Crouching, Carlos hid down beside one of the huge pine trees that formed a natural entrance way to the ranch, disappearing silently in its shadow.

It didn't take more than a few minutes for the rider to draw nearer. Carlos tensed and, as the rider checked his horse by the trees, he launched himself with split-second timing upon the startled man.

The leap took the unsuspecting rider cleanly out of the saddle and he hit the ground hard, with Carlos on top. The man grunted as the air was knocked out of him and the distinctive sound of bone breaking was clearly heard in the gathering darkness.

The others were quickly there, grabbing hold of the captive as Carlos stood.

Someone brought a lamp and they all looked at this terrible Comanchero whose very name sent shivers of fear throughout the border towns. He didn't look much, just a dusty, skinny little Mexican standing there with a busted arm and eyes full of fear.

Carlos spoke to him slowly in Mexican. 'Be careful that you answer the questions this man will ask of you with truth.' He pointed towards Clarence Dunsford. 'If you lie . . . ' He shrugged but the frightened man got the meaning.

'Ask him what will happen to my wife and children,' Dunsford said.

'This man has had his wife and daughters taken by your friends. What will become of them?'

'All the gringo *señoritas* will be sold to the high-ranking army officers and politicians in Mexico City.'

'Who is the leader of this band?'

'Juan Cristobel Huerta.' The man said with some pride.

Carlos knew Huerta. He was hard, almost inhuman, but he was also very greedy for personal wealth; this Carlos saw as hope for Dunsford's family.

'How safe are the womenfolk of this man?'

'No one will dare touch the gringo women; they are worth too much to Huerta.'

Then the captured man looked slyly at Carlos, sensing perhaps his mixed Apache blood.

'The Apache women, they will not be treated so well, they will be used by the men before they are sold.' He said this with a smirk.

'If you were there with them now would you use them also?'

'Of course. Is that not why God put Apache women on this earth, to be mattresses for Mexicans?'

Carlos punched him heavily in the mouth, knocking him backwards. 'You will never use them again *amigo*, and that's for the ones you already have.'

Suddenly Dunsford was there, tugging at his arm. Turning, he found the angry face of the rancher looking at him.

'Well?' Dunsford demanded.

'They are headed for Mexico City where they will be sold. Their leader is a man called Juan Huerta. I know of this man, your wife and daughters are safe from the men in his gang because of their worth to Huerta. None will dare touch them while they are on the trail.'

'What about him?' Dunsford pointed with disgust at the captive.

'It would be wise to hang him. That would make one less we'll have to fight later.'

Dunsford turned to the man next to him; his voice shook. 'Get a rope.'

In ten minutes it was all over. The figure of the Comanchero dangled from a stiff hemp rope thrown over a thick branch of one of the pines, his hands tied behind his back. He still jerked occasionally and stank of urine when his bladder had released itself.

'We are taking only ten men with us; do you think that is enough?'

'No. We would need a hundred to be enough, but ten will have to do.'

'The moon is surely bright enough to follow their trail, why waste any more time?' Dunsford was itching to start.

'Very well.'

They moved off following the tracks

left by the men they hunted, which headed off to the south-west, aiming generally in the direction of the Rio Grande and the Mexican border.

3

Their trail was easy to follow in the clear, brilliant moonlight, which was known as a Comanche moon owing to the fact that the Comanche used the bright light shed at this time of year to send war-parties raiding deep into Mexico. They could travel in the cool of the night and rest up during the heat of the day.

For the first five hours they made good time. Just on dawn Carlos, who had been out scouting, called a halt on the banks of the fast-flowing Big Springs river, and pretty soon a morning camp was set up.

The smell of bacon frying and the rich aroma of coffee on the boil reminded Carlos of just how hungry he was. He saw the big, black horse watered and fed, then got his plate, pannier and cup, along with his vittles, and wandered over to the cooking-fire to prepare his meal.

Dunsford came up as he was piling some beans and bacon on to his plate.

'We'll let the men take their ease for an hour or so, then we'll hit the trail again, I think, Carlos.'

The day would be hot. The heat coming from the plains would get up into the hundreds by mid-morning, sapping the very life energy from man and horse.

'It might pay to do our travelling in the late afternoon, Mr Dunsford; it's the month they call the Comanche moon. The moon will give us plenty of light and we can travel in the cool of the night, rest up during the worst of the day's heat.'

'If you think that's best.' Carlos could see the man was unconvinced. 'As long as we catch them before they cross the Rio Grande and escape into Mexico.

'We'll catch them, Mr Dunsford.'

In the late afternoon they ate the last meal of the day and rested some more in preparation for another night trek, cursing the flies and the heat that was slowly boiling off. After each man had filled his water bottle Carlos got them started once again. There had been no wind or rain to remove the bandits' tracks so, making sure the others could easily follow the trail, he decided to scout ahead.

He'd only ridden a couple of miles before he found one of their abandoned campfires. It was plain to see where they had spread out, corralled the captives and set up three cooking-fires. The fires were long cold, so he knew they had passed this way many hours before. However he was confident that the pursuers would catch them up sometime in the next day or so, if the moonlit nights continued to favour them and the weather held.

But of course it didn't.

Without warning the temperature suddenly dropped. Carlos knew what was coming and turned the stallion's head back toward the others. He reached them in time to yell at the startled men to quickly find whatever cover they could and hunker down. Then, only moments later, it struck with breathtaking force.

The wind, known as the Blue Norther, sweeping unhindered all the way from Canada in the north, released its full, freezing fury upon man and beast. All they could do was cower on the ground as the wind scoured every inch of exposed flesh with abrasive grits of sand, flung at them with enormous force. Despite the bandannas they covered their faces with and the Stetsons they pulled over their ears the sand got everywhere.

Men and animals, most of them for the first time in their lives, found themselves facing nature's wrath, which seemed hell-bent on destroying them.

A desert storm is a formidable, awesome opponent, it asks for no quarter and gives none, whipping sand and debris about and changing the landscape. But a Blue Norther is ten times worse, for it carries ice-charged air. Within fifteen minutes the ground was frozen hard as steel.

They could do nothing except force their mounts to the ground and gather what shelter they could from the trembling, frightened horses.

Several hours later the wind stopped and once again the moon shone down. It was as if nothing had happened.

It took Carlos about an hour to pick up the trail again, though boot-marks and horse-prints were completely gone. However, the thin, parallel wheel tracks had already sunk deep into the ground before it froze over and were still easy to follow.

The trail twisted and turned as they began to enter rocky washes and rugged little hillsides. The killer northerly, now only a bad memory, was replaced by a gentle westerly breeze, blowing softly through the yellow buffalo grass, whispering and sighing as it went.

Carlos realized their quarry was beginning to take more care of how they travelled, trying to hide their movements and obliterate their sign; he figured the men ahead knew they were now entering Apache country. He circled a little to the right and silently signalled for the others to follow.

Many hundreds of years before, an avalanche had left a natural wall of large boulders that led down to a pool of clear water. It was down this trail that he led them.

They eventually came out into a large grassy valley. The country around here often hid such places of rest and peace. A person could ride across the tops of the lava beds or mesas that were devoid of any kind of life except perhaps the odd rattlesnake or Gila monster, then travel down what might appear to be a crack in the surface and fetch up at just such an oasis as the one they now found themselves in.

The men they tracked had been here and gone perhaps as little as a day ago. They had done their best to obliterate their telltale sign but Carlos easily picked it out. He could see where they had built their cooking fires and where they had rested the captives, tying them by their necks to the big wheels of the wagons. Carlos could also tell that they had not stayed here very long.

Every paradise has its serpent and this one was no exception. It manifested itself in the form of deer flies. The little pests not only gave painful bites but, for some reason known only to Mother Nature, they stung when they bit as well. Cursing, slapping, men led bucking, kicking horses to drink.

However, it wasn't long before several of the horses were rolling and snorting happily in the thick green meadow grass, like playful newborn colts.

Carlos, keeping his distance from the others, unsaddled the black and put a hobble on him. This was Apache country and being half-Apache himself, Carlos knew what great horse thieves they were; it was second nature to them, and this magnificent stallion would make any Apache buck's mouth water. From now on he and the men he led must also go with caution, for the Apache, too, could be mean sons of bitches when the mood took them.

Even teach the Comanche a new trick or two.

4

Soon the smell of cooking was in the air and the men started to relax.

Carlos sat apart from the campfire after cooking his meal and filling his cup with strong black coffee. Some of the men were talking quietly together and Clarence Dunsford seemed lost in his own private world of worry and fear over the fate of his family.

Carlos decided to go and talk with him, maybe ease his mind a little, for he was certain that no harm would come to the haunted man's womenfolk while they were on the journey to Mexico City.

As he began to move over to where Dunsford sat the voice of Clem Abbots stopped him short.

'Hey Carlos, is it true the Apaches are scairt of the Comanche?' Carlos took a deep breath, deciding that he would not be drawn into whatever game they had decided to play and, doing his best to ignore the comment, he continued on over to Dunsford.

But Clem just wouldn't let it go.

'Hey Carlos, you son of a bitch, you answer when a white man speaks to you.'

Suddenly he could feel his anger rising. He had lived all his life with such taunts. Being half-Apache, half white was to be never fully accepted into the white man's world, tolerated, even liked by some, but mostly looked down upon.

Even his days of schooling back East had seen him get into fight after fight against those who would not accept him as an equal until he became so handy with his fists that he was eventually left alone.

Left alone but never accepted.

He had friends in the town of Big Springs, good friends but only up to a point. However, his mother's people accepted him without question and embraced him as one of their own.

To his advantage he had applied the skills inherited from his Indian upbringing to the white man's education, an education his father had insisted he should get from an Eastern college from the ages of fourteen to eighteen.

Between both cultures he had done OK.

He owned land bequeathed to his father by the Apache, land on clear title that had good water and grass. His house was solid and warm and his woman was a beauty. Yes, he had done better than a lot of the white men gathered here now waiting to see what he was going to do about Clem Abbots.

Clem was a big, beefy man, and as Carlos approached he climbed lazily to his feet, arms hanging loosely at his side, confident, waiting.

Carlos calmly walked over to where Abbots stood, waiting to be answered. The answer the big man received, however, was not the one he expected. Instead of words, Carlos punched him with a solid left jab that caught him right between the eyes. This was followed by a combination right hook to the jaw, a deep, hurting chop to his stomach. A right uppercut under his chin finished it off.

The big man folded, out for the count.

'Does anyone else want to ask me anything?'

No one said a word. The only sound was the merry hissing of the cooking fire and the soft groans of Clem Abbots slowly recovering.

He found Dunsford lost in his thoughts as he hunkered down beside him. The fight with Abbots was over so quickly that Dunsford hadn't even noticed. The Englishman looked up, suddenly realizing that someone was close to him.

'Without my family there is no point in continuing to build a life in this god-forsaken land,' he mused sadly.

'The land can be good to those who learn to respect it and use it wisely, Mr Dunsford,'

'Oh yes, I daresay you are right. It will grow healthy cattle and horses, but it breeds such violence. In England there are courts and judges and laws and a police force to enforce them. Out here the only law is a gun. A man kills for what he wants and there is nothing to stop him.'

Carlos had no argument to offer him simply because the other man was right. 'Law will come eventually, Mr Dunsford.' He knew his words would offer little comfort to a man who needed help right now, not three or five or ten years in the future.

Dunsford turned to face the tracker square on. In the early light of dusk Carlos could see the anguish in his eyes. 'Will I ever get them back, Carlos, and if I do will they be the same people?'

'Don't give up hope, Mr Dunsford; there's still a fair way to go to the border yet.'

He left Dunsford and walked out of the campfire's glow. Abbots and the others had lost interest in trying to bait him any further and remained angrily silent as he walked past, heading for his sleeping blanket.

He had seen some signs today which he had not mentioned to anyone. Mostly because the signs were of Mescaleros Apache.

There had been about a dozen of them and the tracks were about a day old. A hunting party or a war party? That he didn't know, but he did know they had cut the sign of the Comancheros also and that only added up to a whole new heap of problems. However, Carlos and the men he led had one ace up their sleeve. The Apaches wouldn't know they were behind them, not unless they sent a scout back to their village for reinforcements to fight the Comancheros and that scout blundered into them.

The next morning at breakfast he gathered the group together. Abbots was sullen and quiet. If Dunsford noticed the cuts and bruising on the big man's face he didn't say anything. Throughout the long sleepless night Carlos had formed a plan and he wanted to explain it to them.

'Yesterday I cut Apache sign about three miles to the east.' Well, that was good. The word Apache sure got their attention. 'There are about a dozen of them and they're tracking the Comancheros.'

'Then we have no time to lose.' Dunsford was on his feet in a second, his face draining of colour. 'If my family fall into their hands there'll be no saving them.'

'The Apaches won't attack them outright; there are not enough of them at the moment. My guess is that they'll try to pick off stragglers, steal horses and try to slow Huerta down. He must have something they want, probably Apache women. In the meantime they'll probably send a warrior back to their village for more braves and only then will they attack in force. At the moment they're content to be thorns in his side.'

'So what do you suggest we do? We now have the Apaches between us and the Comancheros. Do we have to go through them before we can attempt a rescue?'

It was plain to see that Dunsford was getting himself all riled up, and who could blame him?

Boscombe spoke up. 'If they're Apache why not go and talk to them, Williams? Get them on our side. Hell, they might even be your kin.'

What the tracker thought of Boscombe's words right then was indicated by his hand suddenly hovering over the butt of the Colt buckled round his lean waist. Harvey's face changed colour and he suddenly knew he was pushing too hard.

'These are not Lipan Apache, you son of a bitch; these are Mescalero, and they're worse than any goddamn Comanche you ever heard of, Boscombe.'

Harvey dropped his eyes, looked away and the charged moment was gone. Carlos turned his attention back to Dunsford.

'I think Huerta will now head for the

town of Presidio, this side of the border. There he can make a stand. If he's successful and beats the Apaches he'll probably head to Chihuahua. When he's sure the Apache have stopped chasing him he'll light out for Mexico City.' As he spoke Carlos picked up a stick and began drawing in the sand.

'The Comancheros are about four days' travel from the Rio Grande and about two days ahead of us. Now, with the Apaches dogging them, they'll be forced to travel faster and cut that down to about three days. I know a pass that we can take through Apache Mountain that will get us to Presidio at least ten or twelve hours before the Comancheros get there. But I warn you all now, it will be hard going on man and horse.'

Dunsford looked unsure. 'Is there no other way?'

'No! We have the Apaches between us and Huerta. If we catch up with them some will turn around and fight us, slowing everything down and Huerta will take that opportunity to escape.'

This time Fes Bishop spoke up putting his nickel's worth in. 'The Apaches will go after the goods and prisoners the Comanchero have. Hell, everybody knows how goddamn greedy they are.'

Carlos took a deep breath forcing the anger down; now was not the time. 'They will have no trouble following Huerta well into Mexico. They've been raiding there for years. Besides, you're forgetting the others that will arrive; we'll be caught between them.'

That thought didn't sit well with any of them.

'The short cut through the mountains will gain us time, and surprise. It's our best shot.'

Carlos sat his horse waiting while they talked among themselves. He had laid it out for them; there was nothing more he could add. It was Dunsford's call now.

Dunsford suddenly made up his mind. 'All right, we don't seem to have much choice. The longer we stand here gabbing about it the further away they're getting. I'll double the amount already promised to any man willing to go on and see this through.'

Most of them were flat-land cowboys. The sight of the mountains they must climb brought fear to their faces that they couldn't hide.

Lying dark and brooding to the west, the highest peak was 7,000 feet or more. They loomed up out of the distant horizon like the backbone of some giant skeletal lizard: dark, forbidding and ominous.

But in the end the likes of Boscombe and his pals were greedy men at heart and the others were genuinely concerned for the women, so none of them offered to quit.

But Carlos knew that it wouldn't be very long before they wished they had.

5

They reached the foothills of the mountains three hours later with about an hour's light left. The men stopped and gathered together, once again talking among themselves and occasionally looking in the tracker's direction.

Dunsford stood apart, his mind on other things, unmindful of the murmurs of the men; he had but one objective.

Carlos began scouting around for the start of the trail that would take them through to the other side when Herb Conroy, one of Jeb Claiborne's riders, approached him.

'Carlos, the men are tired and need a rest. We can pick up the trail at first light tomorrow, can't we? Not too much time will be lost.'

Carlos looked across at Dunsford. The Englishman carried his impatience like a second skin, but a night's rest would see all of them, the horses included, in better shape to handle whatever lay ahead tomorrow.

'Ok, but keep the fires low, Herb, and have them see to their horses.'

Within minutes, a small cooking-fire was burning and Carlos had to admit to himself that he too was hungry. But before going to chow with the others he saw to his horse. When this was done he took his pannier and mug, some bacon and coffee, and a tin of beans, over to the fire to prepare his supper.

After eating his meal he lay down, using his saddle as a pillow, gazed up at the millions of stars overhead and thought about how much he missed his wife.

The morning came soon enough, as it does in the south-west. Almost from complete darkness to instant light in about as long as it takes a man to open his eyes and stretch.

After the men had eaten their bacon and biscuits, washed down with scalding black coffee thick and strong, the horses were saddled and the journey began once again.

At first it was easy going because the morning was cool and pleasant, but Carlos knew with a certainty that it wouldn't last long.

The trail began as an old game track through the junipers, then entered into the rocks. The climb was gradual and easy and the horses took it without too much effort, however, the higher they climbed the steeper became the gradients until eventually each rider was forced to dismount and lead his horse.

Carlos kept them away from ridges even if, at times, that seemed the easiest route. They couldn't afford for any one to be seen against the skyline.

The sun became a demon by mid-morning, beating down relentlessly from a clear, cobalt sky. Its rays bounced off the huge boulders, which reflected the searing heat, doubling its intensity, making it hard to breathe the super-heated air.

Their gaunt faces glistened with

sweat and busy little insects buzzed eyes and nostrils, trying to get at the moisture they found there. The constant motion of waving them away helped wear the tiring men down.

They'd been going at it for about three hours, stopping occasionally for a break and were about a quarter of the way to the top when trouble started.

It doesn't take much under such conditions for trouble to erupt.

The horse of Toby Bennett, another of Claiborne's men, had lost its footing and had stumbled, sliding backwards in some loose shale, knocking Harvey Boscombe, who was following close behind, to his knees. He'd regained his feet, enraged and breathing obscenities.

Everybody had stopped and some of them were watching Carlos to see what he would do. Carlos didn't intend to do anything as it wasn't his hunting party, it was Dunsford's.

He watched Dunsford make his way back toward the arguing men.

'That's enough!' His voice was loud

in the confines of the narrow canyon. He was a man who was used to being obeyed and the tone of his voice shut Harvey and Toby up straight away.

'We have a long way to go to get my family back and we must work together. If I lose them because of the actions of any man here, then I will kill that man outright.'

His words had sting and no one doubted that he meant them. Reluctantly Boscombe grabbed his horse's reins and after making a show of wiping dust from his jeans moved off again behind Bennett.

Late afternoon found them high in the mountains. The men and horses were struggling in the thinner air, but thankfully it was cooler. A man would curse as his foot slipped on the rocky canyon floor, or a horse would stop and only begin to move again when slapped and punched by the cursing man coming up behind.

Another hour and Carlos knew they would reach the site of an ancient

Tularosa Indian village. Here, waiting for them, would be a pure mountain spring, deep, clean, and ice cold. He called a five minute halt and explained to them what awaited not all that further up.

He could tell by the looks on their faces and the spring in their step as they led off again that the thought of cool water had done the trick; even Dunsford had a slight smile on his face.

He let them all go ahead of him, the trail from here led straight to the spring and he knew they couldn't get lost. He lingered behind to check their back trail.

Something glinted in the sun far away in the direction from which they had come.

It was too far away for Carlos to make anything out even through the binoculars he always carried, yet he was sure he had seen something.

Sunlight off a gun barrel?

Perhaps.

Was someone following their back

trail? Comanche or Apache? Maybe he was mistaken, but he'd lived in this land long enough to trust his gut feelings and right now they told him that they were being followed.

The men were already cooking their evening meal when he eventually caught up. The fresh water had restored their spirits and now they laughed and happily exchanged banter, whereas, a short time ago it wouldn't have taken much for a killing to have taken place.

The horses too, had been given a new lease on life and after drinking their fill were busily munching at the sweet grass that grew in a little valley not far from the spring.

The remains of the Tularosa pit houses could be easily seen. The meadow of grass was a legacy of their long lost civilization.

The big black, unsaddled, was turned loose to drink then join the other mounts in the meadow. Carlos cut a couple of slabs of bacon and, with pannier and mug, once again prepared to cook his meal at the cooking-fire now blazing merrily away. He noted with satisfaction that whoever had built the fire had done so in a way that would make it extremely difficult to spot from any direction.

As the bacon sizzled away in the pan he built himself a smoke.

'You know these parts intimately it would seem, Carlos.'

He turned and looked into the face of Clarence Dunsford.

'Yes.'

'This is a hard, unyielding land, Carlos; it gives nothing and takes all.'

'Well, I guess some might see it like that, Mr Dunsford, but look at what it's given us right here.' He pointed at the spring and the meadow.

Dunsford bowed his head in assent. 'I suppose if a man is born to the land it makes a difference; then he knows how to use it, to take from it what he wants.'

Carlos smiled at his words. 'You mean just like the Indians?'

Dunsford's look encouraged the

tracker to go on. 'The Apaches have been living off this land for hundreds of years and before them the Pueblos. Look around you at these ruins. Men farmed here, raised families and crops and animals. It's a good land if you know how to use it.'

'Well, Carlos, perhaps I'll get you to teach me more about this land, once we've rescued my family.'

'And if we don't? There's always that.'

Dunsford stood quiet for a moment before speaking. His words were little more than a whisper and Carlos had to strain to hear them.

'Then I'll curse this land as the devil's own backyard and return to England.'

6

Mid-morning of the next day found them descending the eastern slopes of Apache Mountain. Once they reached the bottom they would find themselves in New Mexico and from there it would be less than a day's ride to the little town of Presidio.

It was time to hold a council of war.

They all gathered under a stand of piñon trees on the eastern slopes of the mountain they had just crossed and there in the shade made their war plans.

'What do you think, Carlos?' Dunsford asked.

'With the Apaches dogging him, Huerta will be busy watching his back. He won't expect an attack coming from where he expects only safety. We wait until he makes it into the town. Once there my guess is he'll try to use the town as a stockade against the Indians.

With luck he'll lock all the captives up in the old church while he attempts to fight off the Apaches. That will be our chance to rescue them. Once he's occupied one of us will sneak in and release the captives, the rest will stay behind and cover our retreat. I reckon we go back the way we came.'

He could see that that last statement didn't win a lot of approval, but there was no other way that it could be. He turned to Dunsford.

'I guess we do it Carlos's way, boys. Who do you want to go with us?'

Carlos knew every man there and knew whom he would want with him at such a time. He also knew whom he didn't.

He selected six who he knew were handy with rifle and pistol. Those chosen did not include Harvey Boscombe and his sidekicks. They would stay and guard the pass at Apache Mountain.

'We'll head for Presidio when it gets dark and hide inside the town. By my reckoning Huerta should arrive some-time early in the morning. In the meantime we should eat and rest.'

As the long daylight hours dragged by Carlos noticed Boscombe and his two sidekicks, Fes Bishop and Clem Abbots whispering together and casting meaningful glances in his direction when they thought he wasn't looking. He knew they were up to something but decided that whatever it was it would have to wait.

At last the coolness of dusk arrived and the noise of weapons being cleaned and checked for ammunition could be heard as those who were going made final preparations for entering the town. Carlos put his bow and quiver over his shoulder.

Those who were going gathered together for a final powwow. 'Mr Dunsford, you come with me. When we find the women you'll need to let your wife know it's you. The rest of you take up positions around us at the church and cover us. Try to stay unseen so they don't suspect we're in front of them, and shoot to kill. Any questions?'

He looked at each grim face. They were scared of what lay ahead. Hell, most of them were only cowboys drawing wages, but not one of them flinched from what he knew he had to do.

And so they headed off. They would return with Dunsford's womenfolk; or maybe not return at all.

Carlos had been to Presidio several times over the years and knew the lay-out quite well. The old church of Santa Teresa was at the northern end of town. It was into this church, a double-storeyed adobe structure with heavy wooden doors, that he was hoping Huerta would secure the captives while he fought off the Indians.

Once he arrived, and if Carlos had figured right, Huerta would be hard pressed by the Apaches dogging him. The townspeople, mostly poor farmers, would stay indoors once they heard shooting. They were no strangers to Indian raids. Comanches had almost wiped the town out on at least two occasions in the last forty years; there would be no trouble from them.

Huerta would probably throw up barricades across the main street at the northern end and try to blunt the Indians' attack. He would probably use his wagons for that purpose. Carlos intended that his band should remain hidden while this was going on. No man must fire too early and lose the element of surprise, for if they were discovered the captives' safety could be compromised.

When they reached the outskirts of the little town they dismounted and left the horses with Pete Munny, the youngest of the men who had taken up the rescue trail.

'Stay awake,' Carlos warned the youngster. 'When we come back we're gonna be in one helluva hurry. Savvy?'

'Sure thing, Mr Williams.'

'If we're not back by noon you skedaddle.'

'Yessir.'

Quietly, on foot, with darkness as

their shield, they entered the little town. They could hear someone playing on a guitar and singing a sad Spanish song. There were a few lights burning in some of the houses, but for the most part the only real light was the moon.

They made their way to the church and after scouting carefully around, took up positions out of sight as best they could and settled down waiting for the morning.

'Carlos, are you awake?' Dunsford's voice was a whisper in the darkness.

'Too damn cold to sleep, Mr Dunsford.'

'When do you think they'll get here?'

He considered this for a while before answering. 'The Apache won't fight Huerta openly at night, but at the same time they'll want to stop him getting somewhere where he can fortify his position, if they can. A lot depends on how many Indians there are and whether they outnumber the Comancheros. My guess would be that the Apaches will attack them at first light and that Huerta will make his dash here then. He'll come in fast and he'll come in hard and he'll be worrying about what's chasing him, not what's already here waiting for him.'

'Well, the plan seems sound enough, so I suppose all we can do now is wait.' Dunsford sighed and looked off into the gloom. 'Jeb Claiborne tells me you have quite a spread of your own, Carlos.'

The younger man didn't mind his talking; it was hard to sleep anyway. 'Yes! My father came West when the Mexican government opened Texas up in 1814 to settlers from the North.'

'From the North? You mean America?'

'Yes! He met my mother after she found him on the trail one day, he'd been bitten by a rattler, and my mother saved his life.'

'Your mother was Apache?'

'Of the Lipan clan. My father had been a doctor back East and he saved many Lipan lives when an epidemic of smallpox struck the village. In return my parents were given the land we now hold to farm and raise cattle. I have carried on in my father's footsteps.'

'Have you registered your land, Carlos? There are many who would seek to take it from you one way or another.'

'You mean because I'm part Indian?' Carlos chuckled softly. 'My land is safe. It is legally registered in town with the bank and I have my own copy squared away safe and sound. No! Mr Dunsford, whoever would try to take my land would have to kill me first and then they would have to kill my wife and her brother.'

'Perhaps when this is over we could look at improving your stock. Most of your beeves are Texas longhorn, are they not? Perhaps we could breed some of the female cattle you have with some of my Hereford stud bulls. I had them shipped out from England two years ago and they're doing really rather well. The offspring carry more meat than a longhorn and the meat is more tender.'

He had a soft, lilting voice and his

English accent took a bit of getting used to but Carlos understood very well what the other was driving at.

That could certainly improve the stock! Carlos had seen some of Dunsford's Herefords and they did carry a lot more meat than the leaner, skinnier longhorn, and it was meat that was in demand up North. Also it might breed some of that longhorn meanness out of them.

However, Dunsford's next words brought him back to reality with an unpleasant jolt.

'Harvey Boscombe: I fear you've made quite a nasty enemy there, Carlos. He's a mean man, a little man who is bitter with his life and envies those who have more than he has. You would do very well to take care around him.'

Carlos had forgotten about Harvey.

'I guess I'll have to worry about that when it happens.' He had to push it away; dawn was not too far off and he needed to concentrate on what lay ahead. Already pastel fingers of light were beginning to poke at the eastern sky.

'I don't think it will be long now.' The words had barely left his lips when faint sounds of gunfire were heard, mingled with the war-whoops of the Apaches.

7

Sometimes in a man's life things come together as planned, and this was one of those rare times. As the dawn light increased, so the battle taking place out on the plains came closer and closer to the little town. Soon the waiting men could see the Comancheros streaming towards the town, fighting a running battle with twenty or so Apaches close on their heels.

The Indians were trying desperately to get in front of Huerta's racing wagons and cut them off. In the fast-growing light the Mexican wagons could be seen bouncing and rearing high in the air, packed with the frightened, screaming captives. These *carrelas* were built to carry heavy weights, not for speed.

Huerta had separated the captives, putting the white women, about seven in number, into one wagon, while in two others he'd placed the captive Apache women. He fought his way closer and closer towards the safety of the town. To those looking on it was almost impossible not to feel the excitement rising. Would Huerta and his men make it?

Then Huerta did something that showed the depths to which he was capable of sinking to save his own skin. Digging cruel Spanish spurs into his panting horse's side and quirting its neck savagely, he raced the flagging beast up beside one of the wagons containing about ten or so young Apache women. Then, using a sharp-bladed machete, he slashed at the traces until they parted. The horses, now free from their burden, continued galloping wildly on while the wagon, no longer controlled, swerved to the side, flipped high in the air and crashed.

Bodies, including that of the driver, flew through the air.

However, it seemed to have the

desired effect for it slowed the Apaches down as they reined in to help their wives and daughters and sisters. Most of the bodies lay still where they had landed.

Then, with howls of anguished rage the Indians once more continued after the Comancheros.

That murderous, cold-blooded act allowed Huerta and his men to gain the town. They thundered into the main street, jumped quickly from their mounts and began to pull the remaining women from the wagons. Indian and white were herded together and Huerta, pointing to the church, sent the women off under the guard of two sweating, cursing men who drove the terrified women with kicks and blows into the church.

With the captives out of the way they proceeded to block the street by overturning the wagons. Some of the horses, those with arrows sticking from their hides, were brought to the front of the overturned wagons and shot where they stood, adding strength to the makeshift barricade.

Carlos took his bow from his back and nocked an arrow. 'I'm going to take those two men guarding the church doors. When that's done get there as fast as you can and bring out the women. Lead them back to the horses and high-tail it out of here the way we came in.'

Dunsford tensed as Carlos sighted up one of the guards, then quickly released the missile. The arrow took the luckless Mexican in the throat and pinned him to the church door where he hung quivering, legs drumming a death tattoo.

The second arrow, launched a split second later, hit the second guard straight through the chest, pinning him to the door also. Just then the rest of Dunsford's men opened fire into the renegades' rear.

Clarence Dunsford was off to the church like a man possessed.

No one had seen what had happened

and now Carlos, his fighting blood fully aroused, was determined to remove a few more Comancheros and their Comanche allies from this world before heading back after the others.

He sneaked along the side of a house, which brought him to a spot where he could clearly see the defenders. Preoccupied fully with the battle and saving their lives, they had no idea that death had come calling from behind.

The third arrow took a scrawny Mexican in the middle of the back and he went down without a sound.

Huerta! Where was the son of a bitch?

Then Carlos saw him. That was at about the same time that one of the Comanche warriors, fighting beside the Mexican bandit, turned and looked straight at Carlos. He quickly brought his rifle up and fired a shot. Wooden splinters flew inches from the young tracker's head. But the Comanche had hurried his aim, and it did no harm. He cranked the lever for a second round but Carlos fired his arrow first and it took the Indian cleanly in the chest.

Huerta must have somehow sensed that there was danger behind him, for suddenly he crouched down and spun round, looking wildly about. This sudden movement took Carlos by surprise and the arrow aimed for his upper torso buried itself harmlessly into a sack of grain someone had dragged over for defence.

But Carlos had been taught well in the art of warfare by an Apache uncle. His next arrow, fired less than a split second later, went under Huerta's right upper arm and penetrated through to the man's black heart.

The Apaches meanwhile were pressing their attack home with single-minded tenacity, and Carlos didn't want to be here when they eventually broke through. He knew they would show no mercy to anyone they found alive, Comanchero, Comanche, or innocent townspeople, maybe even Carlos himself.

He fired three more arrows, killing

two Comanche braves and wounding one Comanchero. Then it was time for him to leave and catch up with the others. It looked as if this particular Comanchero band would never take any more captives or trade again.

He melted away into the shadows, following after the others to where he hoped to find his horse. To his surprise he found Pete Munny waiting with the black stallion.

'Just wanted to make sure you made it back OK, Mr Williams, and that your horse was here waiting for you.'

'Thanks, *amigo*, but we'd better get out of here.'

Suddenly Pete Munny stiffened, his eyes growing large in fear.

'Apaches, Mr Williams?'

Carlos turned. Not fifty feet away were six mounted Apache warriors. Their leader was a man Carlos knew well. Na-ai-che, a Mescalero chief, lifted his hand in salute and Carlos knew they had recognized the markings of his arrows in the bodies of Huerta and the others he had killed.

He returned the salute. 'OK, Pete. Let's ride.'

As the two forked their horses away from Presidio they heard triumphant howls from the victorious Indians and knew that it was all over. It was best not to think about the fate of those who were left alive and in their turn had become captives of the Apaches.

8

Carlos and Pete caught up with the others in the foothills of Apache Mountain. They had stopped and were resting in the shade of some large boulders.

'Carlos. Thank God you made it.' Dunsford got to his feet as the two riders drew near. Carlos and Pete dismounted and shook hands with Dunsford. 'How did it go? Did you get all the women?'

'It went exactly as you planned it. Once you killed those two guards I entered the church and called out to my wife. All the white women came with me but the Indians wouldn't. Here, she's over in the shade with the others, come, I'll introduce you.'

Mrs Dansford was a very beautiful woman, even though her clothes were torn and filthy and her face streaked with grime. Her two daughters stood at her side. Though no judge in these matters Carlos figured them to be about fifteen or sixteen. Both were very pretty, he could see their mother in them.

They looked at him with tired, frightened eyes. It would be a long time before they forgot what they had been through.

'Mr Williams, my husband has told me that we owe our lives and more to you. I just want to thank you for what you've done.' She began to sob.

'Mrs Dunsford, I'm just glad that I could help out.' Carlos turned to Clarence Dunsford, embarrassed to be the recipient of so much gratitude. 'I doubt the Apache will follow us, so we can take it slow going back, let the women rest as much as they can.' He noticed the other four women, just as dirty and frightened as the Dunsford women. 'We'll hand the others over to the sheriff when we get back and he can notify the army.'

However, something that he couldn't put his finger on for the moment began nagging at the tracker. He looked round at the group.

Then it struck him.

'Where's Boscombe?'

'He and his friends volunteered to go ahead to make sure we didn't run into any trouble on the way home.'

Now that sounded just a little too public-minded for Harvey Boscombe. Carlos had never known Boscombe to volunteer for anything.

'We'll rest up and grab some chow, then we'll move further back into the mountains. We'll find a safe spot and set up camp for the night.'

Within minutes they were all mounted up, the women riding double with the men. Ruth Dunsford rode behind her husband, her arms wrapped tightly round his waist. Carlos noticed with a slight grin that young Pete Munny rode with the eldest Dunsford girl behind him. Pete Munny had proved his loyalty and Carlos found himself liking the young cowboy. Perhaps if he needed a job when they got back Carlos might offer him one.

That night Boscombe, Fes Bishop

and Clem Abbots found them.

'We scouted the trail ahead, Mr Dunsford, and it seems to be clear enough. We should be able to make it back to Big Springs day after tomorrow, but me and the boys will ride out again in the morning just to make sure.'

The night passed peacefully enough, except for a few minutes after midnight when one of the women awoke with a scream. The others were quick to surround her offering comfort until, crying softly, she went back to sleep.

True to his word, the next morning Harvey and his friends were up early and, after a breakfas of beans washed down with black coffee, made ready to leave camp.

'We'll make sure the trail's clear through the mountain, Mr Dunsford, then we'll carry on to Big Springs and tell the sheriff to expect you all in a day or so.'

'I appreciate your help in all this. When we get back I'll see that you and the others are well paid.' Dunsford watched as the three rode away, then he came to where Carlos Williams sat finishing his coffee.

'It's probably best that he's gone. It seems I worried about him and you for nothing, Carlos.'

'Men like Boscombe don't forget wrongs, Mr Dunsford, they just postpone the payback for a more convenient time.'

'So you don't think the trouble between you is over?'

'Harvey Boscombe's father and mine came into the territory at the same time. My father's destiny led him on a different trail from that of Jeff Boscombe, Harvey's father.'

Dunsford urged the young tracker to continue.

'Jeff had married a woman from back East and she couldn't take the harsh life in the south-west. After Harvey was born she ran away with a tinhorn gambler, leaving Jeff to raise a son on his own. He did a passable job of starting up a business as a blacksmith, but then he got himself killed by an Apache he'd tried to cheat out of a string of horses. Harvey took over the business and has been a hate-filled son of a bitch ever since.'

'What will you do?'

'If I have to, Mr Dunsford, I'll kill him. He will bring it on himself; that's his way, but somehow, one way or another, it will probably come to that.'

'If there is anything I can do to help you, Carlos, you only need to ask.'

'I'm obliged, Mr Dunsford, but your major concern is rebuilding what you had and taking care of your family.'

Shortly after their conversation the group started off again. Carlos decided that he would remain behind, giving the rest of them a few hours start. This would enable him to check the back trail, just on the off chance that they were being followed. The person whom he thought he had seen following them on the way in had not shown his hand, maybe never would, but Carlos hated mysteries, so he would bring up the rear.

He waited until the sun was high, then started following the others.

It didn't take long before the heat was like an oven and it would be several hours of climbing in it before he reached the cooler altitude. He constantly swept his gaze around the shimmering horizon from left to right and frequently stopped to check behind.

The trail he had led the rescue party over had been steep in places and sometimes there was little more than an animal track leading around a cliff wall, with sharp drops off the side. One faulty step and horse and rider would be over the edge sliding into oblivion.

It was in just such a place that the attack came.

No rifle shot rent the air; just the faintest scrabble of small rocks falling and then the sudden, roaring avalanche of rocks and shale gathering momentum. The wall of detritus pushed his horse over the edge. At first the gallant stallion rode down the moving, sliding slope on his haunches but his plunging got faster and faster.

Carlos pulled his legs free from the stirrups just as the horse slipped sideways and began to tumble end over end.

Jumping free of the saddle he tumbled down behind his stricken mount, hitting his head on a rock. As he did so he lost consciousness; the last sound he heard was the terrified screams of his dying horse.

Sometime later he regained his senses. It took a little while for him to remember what had happened. He tried sitting up, gazing around, but the instant throbbing in his head made him lie down again. He found he was buried waist deep in shale and scree and his left leg was jammed.

Despite the pain, he forced himself to sit up once again. It was then that he realized that his left arm was hanging broken at his side. Though he wouldn't cry out, the pain the effort of movement cost was excruciating. But at least he had been able to take stock of his situation.

It wasn't good.

The horse lay dead about ten feet in front of him, his neck at a queer angle and his shiny black coat splattered in dust and blood.

Carlos owed his life to that big black horse.

By falling and tumbling ahead of his rider, the momentum of his 1,500 pound bulk had pushed the scree into a heap in front of him, eventually slowing him down and Carlos also.

Yes, the horse had saved him for the moment, but unless he could free himself and move into the shade it would be for nothing.

The sun was beating down mercilessly, and he knew that he must try to move somehow. If he didn't the sun could burn the eyes out of his head. Also, thirst would eventually be a problem: his biggest problem.

He struggled to free his legs, sweat running freely down his face, stinging his eyes until he couldn't see through the blur of tears. He had to stop; all the struggling was getting him nowhere, just using up valuable energy and increasing his growing thirst.

The horse had fetched up against the base of a large rock but it was too far away from the wounded man to do him any good. He could plainly see the canteen still attached to the saddle and the thought of the water it contained gave him strength for another try at freeing himself.

With an effort born of desperation he heaved back on his right elbow, digging it into the shale behind and at the same time trying to draw his legs up, then pushing forward with them to gain some sort of leverage.

He almost screamed, as white-hot pain coursed up through his left side and he realized the grim truth: his left leg was broken also.

He had no protection from the sun for his head; his hat lay twenty feet away on the slope. Gingerly he removed the leather jerkin he wore, then, using his right hand he unbuttoned his shirt and somehow got the torn and bloodied garment free. He draped it over his head; at least it might keep out the worst of the sun's rays. He guessed it was about one o'clock in the afternoon. The day wouldn't start to cool down for at least another three or four hours.

He must have dozed for the sound of rustling feathers brought him back to reality with a start.

A large, bald-headed buzzard, its wrinkled skin-flap hanging thick and scaly beneath its wicked-looking beak, fixed the badly hurt man with a black-eyed stare from beside the dead stallion, while more of its friends circled above. Carlos, somehow finding some strength from somewhere, picked up a small rock and though the effort cost him considerable pain, threw it at the big bird. With a savage squawk the carrion-eater was airborne once again, but Carlos knew that he had only delayed the inevitable. The bird and his friends could afford to wait; they had all the time in the world.

The time passed slowly and he began to feel light-headed.

His thoughts began to wander to his home and to Nadie. He could see her before him, calling him to come into the house for supper. He could plainly see himself, stripped to the waist, washing down in crystal-clear, icy-cold water before going in to eat.

There was beef and corn, potatoes and home-baked bread on the table. She called to her brother to wipe his feet before coming into the house. Then he heard her calling him again. Why was she calling him still when he was already sitting at the table? And, what was even stranger, why was her voice so very far away when she was only sitting across from him.

'Carlos. Carlos, wake up.'

He felt his head lifted and water trickled down his throat. He choked, gasping for air but pulling the canteen back to his mouth when it was taken away.

'Carlos.'

He opened his eyes and looked directly into the face of his wife. He had never put too much faith into the teachings of religion but for a moment there, just coming round, he thought that he had died and now he was meeting an angel who looked just like his wife.

However, the sudden pain he felt in his leg as she tugged at him soon brought him back to reality. 'Nadie!'

'I followed you.'

'Then it was you I saw on our back trail.'

'I didn't trust some of those men and I was right. I watched them start the rockslide that knocked you off the mountain trail. It was the blacksmith and two other men.' Apaches never used people's given names if they could help it, it was part of their superstitious culture, but Carlos sure as hell knew who Nadie meant.

'You saw them?'

'Yes. I have been trailing you ever

since you left five days ago. I have been keeping well out of sight and early this morning I saw the blacksmith and two others hide themselves in the rocks overlooking this trail. Several hours later a group of riders, men and women, came through also. They never saw the men hiding above them and they all rode past unmolested. You were not among them and I guessed you were watching the back trail. I'm sorry, my husband, but by the time I realized they were setting a trap for you, you had walked right into it before I could warn you.'

She poured more water into his mouth as she spoke.

'When the dust from the slide had settled, the blacksmith and his friends rode away. I think they believed you were dead.'

'Well, they sure got that wrong.'

It didn't take long with Nadie's help to get free of the shale. She hunted around and found some thick branches of a juniper tree from which she made splints for his busted leg and arm. The slide the horse and rider had taken had more or less left a clear path of shale back up to the point from which they'd been forced off.

Nadie tied a rope under her husband's arms, then took the end back up that path to where her own horse waited.

As she couldn't pull the wounded man straight up the slope, she took the rope round a boulder that seemed large enough to take his weight. She then tied the loose end to her horse's saddle and slowly urged him forward along the trail above.

It worked! Without too much effort Carlos found himself slowly moving backwards, inch by painful inch, to safety.

9

At last he gained the trail and with much painful effort from Nadie and himself, he managed at last to climb into the saddle. Nadie slipped easily up behind him and they headed off back towards their home.

There would be time left after his wounds healed to deal with Harvey Boscombe.

He wouldn't remember much about the painful, two-day trip back to their ranch; most of the time he slipped in and out of consciousness aware for moments only of stopping now and then when Nadie checked his wounds and poured precious water down his throat, or when they camped for the night and he was painfully pulled from the saddle.

But at last they made it home and with the help of Nairn he was put to bed. When at last he opened his eyes it was dark. He felt Nadie beside him and reached out to touch her. Miraculously his head felt clear and he was surprised to find he was feeling mighty hungry, a sure sign that he was well on the mend.

Nadie stirred. 'So you are awake at last?'

'How long have I been sleeping?'

'This is the third day since we got back home.'

He pulled himself into a sitting position in the bed. 'Has anything happened?'

'Shhh! Nothing has happened. Nobody has been here. My brother went into town yesterday and the talk spread by the blacksmith is that you were killed by the Apaches who trailed you into the hills after the man whose family you rescued and the others got away. The feeling in town is bad against the Apaches. My brother was threatened by some men so he returned here rather than start any trouble. He has told no one that you are still alive.'

'Nairn must stay away from town. Boscombe blames the Apaches to take the focus from himself. But until I can prove otherwise your brother won't be safe.

'Nadie, in the morning you must go to the Dunsfords and ask Clarence Dunsford to come back here with you. We will explain what has happened and he can tell the sheriff. That should stop any more talk of war against the Apaches. In the meantime, woman, if you want me to get well quickly you need to feed me.'

She slipped out of bed, beautiful in the moonlight streaming through the bedroom window. He felt the sudden burning of desire grow. 'Don't be too long, it's not just food this cowboy needs.'

'You must be getting better; now I can stop worrying about you.' She laughed as she went to the kitchen. He heard her light the lamp and begin pushing around pots and pans. Soon the smell of flapjacks, bacon and coffee wafted through the air.

Within minutes he heard the front door open, then came Nairn's voice. 'Bacon, coffee, he gets well then? But still, he is a sick man, he cannot eat that much. Perhaps he needs help; it is the least I can do for my brother.'

Then, without warning all hell broke loose. The sound of many gunshots tore through the air. He heard the windows in the kitchen shatter as volley after volley were poured into the room from unknown gunmen firing from outside.

It continued for what seemed an eternity as Carlos struggled to get out of bed and throw himself on the floor. Then, as suddenly as it had begun, the shooting stopped. He could hear distinctly the sound of horses milling around, heard a muffled curse. Then a flaming arrow was fired through the broken window into the kitchen wall. The unseen men could be heard galloping away into the night.

He began a slow cautious crawl into the kitchen, calling for Nadie, grabbing his gunbelt and pistol off the foot of the bed as he did so.

But the sight that met his eyes filled him with horror and panic. Amid the growing flames lay the blood-splattered, bullet-ridden bodies of his wife and her brother.

That they were dead was beyond doubt. Nothing could have survived that sustained volley, the dozens and dozens of bullet holes through the walls bore witness to the ferocity of the attacks, but he had to be certain. If there was a flicker of life in either of them he could not and would not leave them to the flames. Frantically he crawled from each one in turn, shaking them roughly and seeing his worst fears realized. They were dead.

The flames were beginning to take hold and if he too didn't wish to die in there he needed to escape this rapidly growing inferno that was once his home. Tears blurred his vision as he crawled to the kitchen door and opened it, dragging himself through into the coolness of the night beyond.

He cursed and railed against his inability to move properly. He was little more than a helpless cripple, useless and broken, who could only watch in growing horror and shock as the roaring flames became the funeral pyre for those he loved most in the world.

A veil of coldness dropped down over his soul and he knew the one purpose left in life now was to take vengeance on those who had done this to him. He knew without doubt who it was, no matter how much they meant it to look like the work of Indians.

Obviously thinking him dead, Harvey had come back to finish off any loose ends that might get in his way to lay claim to the ranch.

In his crawl across the yard away from the blazing ranch house he had seen Apache war arrows lying here and there.

The Apaches would get the blame from a frightened and angry town and everyone, ranchers and townsfolk alike, would join forces and declare war on the Apache.

Well, Boscombe had made a fatal mistake: he'd failed to kill Carlos a second time. He'd been sloppy and that was typical of the man. He should have taken the time and effort to make sure of his handiwork back there in the mountains.

That mistake would cost him dearly.

For the rest of the night Carlos softly sang the Apache death chant for his wife and her brother, as his home burned down to the ground.

'Only the mountains live for ever, only the rocks live for ever . . . '

In the early morning light he found himself a strong, round branch from one of the fruit trees in the yard and broke it off. Using the stick as a crutch to lean on he began looking around the yard for more sign.

The spent arrows were of the Lipan Apache, the people of his mother and his wife, Nadie. The distinctive arrow-fletching and the red-and-black markings and nock details left no doubt.

However, there was something strange in the prints made by the horses. The horses had all been shod and one of them had a deep crack in the shoe of its front right hoof that left a distinctive imprint in the soft earth of the yard.

As the attackers had run all the horses off, Carlos had no choice but to use Shanks's pony. But at least, now he had a crutch, and he would use it to walk back to his wife's people. Without another backward glance he started south-west, back towards the distant mountains.

They found him a lot sooner than he expected. Five of them sat their war ponies waiting for him to look up and see them. Limping, shuffling along, he almost walked into them.

'Where is your wife?'

'She is dead.'

'And what of her brother?'

'He is dead also.'

'We saw the flames from your ranch as we were hunting.'

'Yes! They burned everything.'

'Who did this? The Comanche?'

'No! It was white men from the town. They have made it to look like it was the Apache that did this thing.'

'Do they seek to make war?'

'They will do so if they are not informed of the truth. They will bring the soldiers in from Fort Worth.'

'What do you intend to do, Little Brother?'

Carlos looked up into the face of Two Eagles Claw, the elder brother of Nadie. 'Brother, I would stay with my Apache family until I am healed; then I will hunt and kill the ones responsible.'

'It is good that you do this, Little Brother.'

They helped him on to the back of a pony and he rode back to their village clinging desperately to the shoulders of the rider, Single Arrow.

For the first few days he was in a high fever. He didn't recall much other than seeing Nadie from time to time, sitting beside him, wiping his brow with cool water and forcing Apache medicinal liquid down his throat. When at last he came to, after the fever broke on the third day, he saw with sadness that the Nadie of his fever was in fact, Leosanni, Nadie's younger sister.

His stay with his Apache family was one of pain and sorrow. Pain because he forced himself to walk weeks before he should have, and sorrow because everything he did he did without Nadie, knowing that this was how it would be from then on.

Leosanni wouldn't let him out of her sight, and though she took his breath away at times because she looked so much like her dead sister, she couldn't replace her and he found himself unthinkingly pushing her away.

He had only one thought, consuming him like the flames that had consumed his wife: revenge.

Eventually, the time arrived when he no longer needed the aid of a stick to walk. His arm and leg had healed well, the breaks being clean and simple ones.

For the next week he practised with his Colt. He'd always been pretty slick on the draw but now he practised again and again, honing, perfecting, until that gun filled his hand in a blur of speed too fast for the eye to follow.

'You will hunt these killers of my sister and brother?' It was the Apache way that now Nadie's and Nairn's names would never be spoken aloud again, for it was believed that dead bodies no longer held the spirit that was once in them and to speak the dead person's name was to bring their ghost back.

They were sitting on top of a ridge watching the setting sun throwing fiery, purple, and orange and deep red colours across the western sky.

'Yes. I will hunt these men and kill them for what they have done.'

She looked at him. So beautiful in the last of the sun's rays. Her raven hair was shining and sleek. 'When you have done this thing — after, I mean — what will you do?'

He was silent for some time and she thought she had offended him. But he hadn't thought that far ahead. He hadn't allowed himself to think of a future. He had no future; it had been violently taken from him. 'I don't know.'

'Maybe you will come back here and live among us?'

He could find no words to answer that. Quickly he stood. 'Come, it is time we went back.'

When at last he felt strong enough to travel he went to Nadie's father, Owl Talker.

'Father, the time has come when I must take up the trail that leads to sorrow for my enemies.'

The old chief looked at Carlos with much sadness. He too had loved his daughter. 'You are a man whose heart of flesh has been replaced with one of stone. I wish you much success on your quest to find these killers. If, however, you are not successful then I will take the same trail and many white-eyes will die.'

He looked away into the distance.

Carlos felt an anger burn within him. Owl Talker had led his people well over the years. He had always opted for peace with the white men who came like plagues of locusts through his land, always taking but never asking.

They had taken the land that was good, declaring it their Manifest Destiny to do so.

Other Apache clans had fought them while Owl Talker had chosen to lead his people into the hills where he hoped the land would not be found pleasant enough for the white men to desire.

Now the death of his daughter and son had changed that and the old man was prepared to make war. History would see him as just another bloodthirsty redskin, but Carlos saw him as an old man pushed to the limit of his patience, and mourning for his children.

'Is there anything you need, my son?'

'A good horse and pack animal, rifle, some food and water is all that I require.'

'It is done. Ride well and shoot straight,

and I hope we may meet again.'

They gave him a big, raw-boned sorrel, one that would travel for ever if looked after properly, and a packhorse that was also strong and broad-backed. All the gear he needed had been packed carefully. Carlos suspected Leosanni had done this.

The whole village came out to see him ride away. They stood in silence but he knew that they wished him well, each and every one of them. He feared for them, feared for the young bucks. What would become of them when they would no longer be allowed to ride as free as the wind through the land that was as wild as they were? Also he feared for Leosanni. He had grown closer to her than he really cared to admit.

10

The first stop would be his ruined home.

Though reduced to ashes it was still his home. However, he decided to take his time getting there, for he was in no real hurry, not looking forward to what he knew awaited him.

The journey took two days. Two days that allowed him to think and plan what he intended to do. There really wasn't much to plan. He would hunt down Boscombe, Bishop and Abbots and blast them into oblivion.

They would never live to enjoy what they had murdered to get.

He pushed the gelding into the yard; the big horse was skittish, not liking the stink of the burnt remains of timber and human life. Carlos got down from the saddle and slowly walked towards what used to be his house.

It had been a good house, solid and strong, built by his father out of logs he had cut and trimmed himself. It had stood defiantly through many a boiling Texas summer and equally freezing winter. But now? Everything was gone except the chimney which was still standing, pointing at the sky in silent accusation.

It didn't take long to find that which he reluctantly sought. Two hours later he had buried the charred bones of his wife and her brother. He buried them together under the apple tree that Nadie had nagged him to plant six years before. Their common grave looked out over the badlands to the West, a land they had loved.

Now, with that grisly task over, he scoured the yard looking at the sign that had been left. He plainly saw where a group of men had come here a day or two after the attack.

His guess was that it had been Boscombe, and that he had brought the sheriff and a posse out here to see the Apaches handiwork and showing himself to be concerned for what had taken place.

Once again he saw the horse-print, the one with the gap and the missing nail.

Something told him that the print didn't belong to Boscombe. He was a big, beefy man and that print had been made by a horse carrying only medium weight. Bishop or Abbots? No, Abbots too was a big man. Bishop then? But wait. If it were any of them surely he would have noticed that print on their mission to save the Dunsford women? And Harvey, being a blacksmith and all, surely would mend his own horse's shoe? Harvey had grown up in this land also and knew the dangers of ending up with a lame horse.

No! There were others involved, but who in God's name were they?

His next plan was to pay a call on Dunsford and discuss the situation with him. Travelling with him on the trail to rescue his family Carlos had discovered that he was a good man and had grown to like him.

The Strand lay about twenty miles to the east, so by setting off now he would make it by late afternoon. He took one last look around. Whatever happened in the next few days he knew one thing was certain: there were going to be some more graves dug.

As he drew closer to The Strand the rock-strewn, sterile land that acted like a natural border between the two properties slowly began to give way to grass-covered rolling hills and meadows. He rode at a steady trot that quickly ate up the miles but didn't tire the horses. The gelding and the pack-horse were Indian animals, grass-fed and able to travel for many miles without hardship, unlike the cornfed mounts the white men rode, which quickly lost their stamina in a hard land such as this when asked to give more than a short gallop.

From some distance away he began to see the beginnings of a new ranch house well under construction, but from what he could see, there didn't seem to be anybody working on the skeletal structure at the moment.

However, he had little time to ponder this fact for when he reached the two trees where he'd jumped the Comanchero so long ago a bullet whistled inches past his head.

Quickly he dismounted and took shelter behind the thickest of the trees as another bullet thudded into the trunk. He tried to see where the shooting was coming from, a third shot and he spotted the grey wisp of gun-smoke.

Whoever was shooting was doing so from behind a pile of lumber stacked in the yard. There was no way he could cover the distance between them without getting shot as the ground was devoid of any cover. There was only one option that he could see.

'Hello the house.'

'What you want, you bushwhacking bastard?'

He instantly recognized the voice.

'Pete! Pete Munny, it's me, Carlos Williams. Hold your fire.'

'You lying son of a bitch. Carlos is dead.' Three quick shots thudded into the tree, proving the shooter was unconvinced.

'Pete, for God's sake hold your fire. I'll step out from behind this tree and walk towards you. If I'm not who I say I am then shoot me.'

'You better not try anything funny, mister. Now step out easy like and keep yer hands up and away from your gun.'

Slowly Carlos stepped out from behind the bullet-ridden tree and began to walk towards the voice. He hadn't taken more than a dozen steps when the shooter stood up, at the same time lowering his rifle. 'Mr Williams, it *is* you. Christ, we all thought you was dead.'

'Well, Pete, as you can see I'm very much alive. Where's Mr Dunsford?'

Pete's face went pale and he looked shaken. 'Mr Dunsford was killed two weeks ago, ambushed on his way back from town by the damned Apaches.'

'How do you know? Did anyone see the attack?'

'No! His body was found by Jeb Claiborne on the trail. He'd been shot in the back by an Apache arrow and scalped.'

This began to stink to high heaven. Carlos knew for a fact that the Apache hardly, if ever, resorted to scalping a victim. 'Pete, is that arrow still around?'

'Yeah, I guess. I think the sheriff took it back to town as evidence.' He looked away, searching for words. 'I'm sorry to hear the Indians burned you out and murdered your wife and her kin.'

'Well, sometimes it doesn't pay to believe all you hear.'

'Yessir,' Pete Munny was puzzled. 'But Mr Boscombe swears he seen them attacking your ranch. Least that's what he told the sheriff.'

'Pete, has Boscombe been out here at all?'

'I don't think so. Leastways I ain't seen him out here.'

'What about Mrs Dunsford? How is she?'

Munny shrugged resignedly. A wistful look crossed his face.

'I think she's going to take her daughters back to England. She doesn't want to stay here any more. Sold the place lock, stock and barrel to Lars Beauchamp, and went into town.'

'Lars Beauchamp.' Carlos pointed at the half finished house and added. 'What about that?'

'Mr Beauchamp is sending some men out later in the week to finish building. He's planning on living here himself. In the meantime he's paying me to look after it.'

'Pete, I'm going to ride over to see Jeb Claiborne. I don't want anyone to know that I'm still alive, not for the moment anyway. Can I trust you to keep quiet?'

The young cowboy looked puzzled, and then shrugged. 'Sure, Mr Williams.'

11

He approached Jeb Claiborne's ranch with a lot more caution than he had Dunsford's, fully expecting a shot to blast from a window or doorway but all remained silent.

But where were the ranch hands?

And then he found him. Claiborne was lying in the back yard and by the look of him he'd been there for over a week. An Apache arrow protruded from his belly, so at least Carlos knew that Jeb had been facing his killers. Jeb too, had been scalped.

He dismounted and began to read the signs in the yard. There had been about ten riders and, once again, unless the wild Apaches had taken to riding shoed horses, this had not been an attack by Indians. Of course the horses could have been stolen, but he doubted that when weighed up with everything else.

The Apaches would have been more inclined to torture their victim, such as suspending them head first over a slow-burning fire. They would have burned down the house and buildings and pulled down the corrals in a token effort of removing all traces of the hated whites.

Now that was another puzzling matter. Carlos's ranch had been destroyed by fire, razed to the ground. Much sign of Apache had been left behind. Dunsford's new ranch building had been spared. However, Dunsford himself had been killed apparently by Indians. The arrow in his back and the scalping was hard to argue with, least-ways that's how others would see it.

Now here was Jeb Claiborne killed, more or less in the same manner: shot with an arrow and scalped like Dunsford, but his property spared the torch. It was almost as if someone was being selective in what was and wasn't destroyed.

Now only a white man would think that way, an Indian would just simply burn the house down.

He began to look at things in a different way. Harvey Boscombe didn't have the brains or the grit to be trying to take over all the ranch land in the county. Carlos could see him perhaps doing the ambushing, the attacks and killings, but the overall planning of such a grand scheme was beyond the imagination of the blacksmith.

There must be someone else involved, someone with a dream, someone who had seen the attack on Dunsford's ranch by the Comancheros as a trigger to getting everything. But who?

Well, he meant to find out.

He looked at what his best chances were to help bring this about. No one, other than Pete Munny, knew that he was still alive and that was about the only ace he held in this hand of death that had been dealt him.

He needed to head into town and find Sheriff Henry Dodds, see if he had any new information. He figured his best move would be to travel unseen, so that meant travelling at night; the longer he could keep the fact hidden that he was still alive the better.

After burying the old rancher it was time to take the ride into town. He travelled slowly; not wanting to push the horses because the terrain over which they now rode was broken and rocky. The ride, however, gave him time to think.

First the attempt on his life by Boscombe back at the mountains. That could have been retaliation for the years he had envied Carlos, in his twisted, jealous hatred, or for the act of splitting his skull with the pistol; maybe that had been the last straw.

But would Boscombe sink so low as to kill a woman in her own home? Carlos wouldn't put it past him, but surely the blacksmith would have stopped there. The gaining, at last, of the Williams land surely should have been enough for him.

Someone else had seen the opportunity to claim everything by next killing

Dunsford and then Jeb. If he got title to all that land he would become the biggest rancher in the state.

That sort of plan was too ambitious for Harvey, Carlos was sure of it. No matter how you cut it, someone else was the brains behind it all.

Two hours later he reached the town of Big Springs. It was late and most decent folks were in bed. Occasionally a voice could be heard raised in laughter from the Shot Glass saloon. He quietly made his way to the sheriff's office. With a sigh of relief he saw a lantern light burning inside and within two more minutes he had dismounted, tied his horses to the hitching rail out front, knocked on the door and had been admitted by a surprised but obviously pleased Sheriff Dodds.

'Carlos! God, man, they said you was dead.'

'How's the coffee, Henry? I could sure do with a cup.'

Sitting opposite him behind his oak desk, steaming cup of strong, black coffee in his hand, Carlos told the lawman what had happened from the moment he had led Clarence Dunsford and the posse after the Comancheros.

Dodds listened quietly, not interrupting until Carlos began to put his theories forward regarding Boscombe.

'Boscombes's dead, Carlos. Injuns got him about five days ago, just after Jeb. Seems he was headed out to your old spread to lay claim to it as you have suspected. Apaches caught up with him before he got there.'

Now that knocked the wind out of Carlos's sails, but then it dawned on him. Harvey Boscombe had outlived his usefulness. There was no way that he was going to be allowed to have a slice of the land pie. This made it all the more simpler. All they had to do now was see who ended up with the three ranches and then they would have their mastermind. He put that to Dodds.

'I'm afraid it's not going to be that easy, Carlos. The buyers are a consortium from up Kansas way. Strangers, they didn't know Dunsford or Claiborne, or even Boscombe for that matter.'

'It's too pat, Henry.' In his agitation Carlos stood up and angrily paced the office, his boot heels ringing on the wooden floor. Sheriff Dodds sat there, watching him pacing back and forth for a few moments. 'Carlos, it looks like Boscombe did most of the killing trying to put it on the Apaches. I can see that. But surely that would be the end to it all? Boscombe did it all through greed and revenge.'

Carlos wasn't buying it. 'Was he found with an Apache arrow in him and was he scalped?'

Henry Dodds thought about that for a moment. 'Why yes, he was, dammit, he was.'

'There's someone else, Henry, there has to be. Comanches, Pawnee and Sioux will take scalps but not the Lipan Apache.' Carlos punched his right fist into his open left hand emphasizing his point.

'We need proof, Carlos. We just cain't

go ahead accusin' these strangers, this consortium, of bloody murder.'

'You're right. Henry, what about Bishop and Abbots?'

'They lit a shuck outa town, out of my jurisdiction, just before Boscombe was found.'

'Well, I guess that's where I have to start, tracking those two varmints down and making them talk.'

'They're probably well over the border into Mexico by now, son.'

'I don't think so, Henry; I believe I'll start my search for them in Kansas. Maybe Abilene.'

'Kansas? But that's where the consortium . . . ' He stopped and looked at Carlos, a smile playing around the corner of his mouth, but there was no mirth in it.

'I cain't help you, son, as I said it's out of my jurisdiction, but I can deputize you to find them and bring them back.'

Carlos was thoughtful for a few moments 'Well, I guess it doesn't matter who knows I'm alive now, Henry, with Boscombe being dead. The other two will know soon enough when I catch up with them.'

The lawman pondered that for a while before replying: 'Yep! I guess you're right. Tell you what, Carlos. Stay here tonight and get some rest, you sure look like you could use it. Tomorrow we'll go and see Lars down at the bank. See if he can give us help with any names.'

A few minutes later, armed with some old, heavy, ex-cavalry blankets, Carlos made up a bunk in an empty cell. Henry was right; he sure was tired. He was asleep almost immediately his head touched the rolled-up blanket he used as a pillow.

The next morning the smell of strong coffee brewing and bacon frying brought him pleasantly awake. For a few moments he lay there thinking she'd soon come in with a tray. Then the nightmare of reality was instantly back and the truth hit him again like a Comanche war club.

She was never coming back and he was waking up in the jailhouse of Big Springs with a knot of fear, anger and loss in his gut that would probably be his constant companion for the rest of his life.

He threw the blankets aside and sat up from the bunk, suddenly not hungry, only anxious to be up and doing.

''Mornin', Carlos.'

Henry Dodds poured coffee as Carlos entered the office from the cell quarters.

''Morning, Henry. What time is it?'

'It's a little after nine. As soon as Lars opens up we'll go over and see him. In the meantime you better get some grub inside you.'

Though not hungry Carlos knew the older man was right, he had to eat, he couldn't just exist on anger and revenge. He would need all the strength he could muster before this hell was over. He sat down and took the plate of bacon and beans the sheriff offered him. 'You still manage to ruin good food, Henry?'

Henry laughed. 'Well I guess some things never change, Carlos, but at least it's hot.'

'Do you think Lars will tell us who these men are who are buying up all the land, this so-called consortium?'

'I don't know, but I cain't think of anyone else who might help.'

'Henry, has there been any strangers move into town recently?'

'No! Everyone here has been here for years. The only . . . what you might call recent . . . folks was the Dunsfords. Carlos, what if it was the Injuns all along? What if you read the signs wrong? You weren't feeling none too healthy yourself. Maybe you're wrong.'

Carlos stood up quickly and began to pace again. He had thought about this. What if he had been wrong? What if, with his wounds and fever and loss, he had been wrong? But he knew he hadn't. The arrows were Lipan, the nearest Apache tribe in the county and Carlos knew for certain it wasn't them.

'I know the arrows weren't fired by

any Indians and I saw nothing of any warlike behaviour while I was in their village.' He reflected for a few moments. 'I guess it doesn't matter now that people know I'm alive.'

'No, but they might not be all that happy to see you though, Carlos, considering you're — ' The sheriff stopped suddenly, looking out of the window.

'What, Henry, that I'm half Apache? The town's known that all my life.'

'That's true, Carlos, but the town ain't had this kinda trouble before. All I'm saying is don't expect a warm reception from people you might have thought of before as friends.'

'Does that include you, Henry?'

'Shucks, Carlos. I've known you ever since you was too danged small to look over the side of your pappy's buckboard when he brought you into town. No, son, it doesn't include me but it might include Lars Beauchamp. He's opening up now; you ready? Oh, I almost forgot.' The sheriff opened a drawer and took out a tin star.

'Here, pin this on.'

Carlos did so and Henry Dodds swore in him as deputy of Big Springs. Both men then left the jailhouse and headed over the dusty street to the bank.

12

'I'm sorry, Sheriff, Carlos, but I'm afraid I can't let you have their names. It's privileged information.'

'Mr Beauchamp, these men are probably killers. You owe them nothing.'

'Carlos, I believe that the Apaches were responsible for those dastardly attacks on yourself and Dunsford and Claiborne, and even poor Harvey. Why, it's commonly held knowledge here in town.'

'Why would the Apache attack my spread and kill their own people. My wife was of the tribe that's getting the blame.'

'It must have been a different tribe, then, Mescaleros or Chiricahua, there's so blasted many. Anyway, I'm told Indians aren't too particular about who they fight as long as they *can* fight, and the damned Apache is the worst of the lot. This land won't be safe until they're all gone, wiped out to a man.'

Carlos had never had much to do with Lars Beauchamp, apart from regularly depositing the money he made from the army by supplying them with horses, in the man's bank. He was aware that his money sitting right now in a deposit box in this very bank amounted to about $80,000 and he thought, as he listened to the banker's words, of his Indian wife and her Indian brother. They had all had a hand in making that money.

As long as there were people like Beauchamp thinking that way there would never be peace in this land. He stood suddenly. 'I reckon I'll be on my way, I've got a long way to go. But before I go, Mr Beauchamp, I'd like to withdraw all my money. You see, it belonged to my wife and I would hate to think of it sitting in there dirtying up your good white money.'

'Now see here, Carlos,' the banker blustered, looking at the sheriff for moral support.

None however was forthcoming.

Carlos dropped his hand to hover meancingly over the butt of his Colt. 'That's Mr Williams to you, and I'd thank you if you could make that withdrawal now. As I said, I'm suddenly in a hurry.'

Lars Beauchamp, suddenly frightened by this angry young man standing threateningly before him, hurried over to the safe and spun the lock. He counted out a huge pile of notes and brought them over. 'I need you to make out a withdrawal slip, Carlos, er, Mr Williams, so everything is legal.'

Carlos signed the withdrawal slip and looked accusingly at the banker. 'If I find you are covering up for the men who killed my family, or had any part in it yourself, I will kill you.'

His words made an impact on the other man and he suddenly looked frightened, though he tried to cover it up quickly with more bluster.

'Even so I cannot divulge their private details, just as I wouldn't divulge yours or anybody else's.'

'Well, I admire your integrity, Mr Beauchamp; I hope you don't have to die for it.'

After they left the bank and the money had been safely put into his saddle-bags, Carlos climbed into the saddle and looked down at Henry Dodds.

'Well, Henry, this star sure looks out of place on this Indian's chest.'

'It looks OK to me, son. By the by, what trail you intending to take to Kansas?'

'I'll go by the old Chisholm Trail; it will probably be easiest seeing as how I'm not pushing a herd of Texas longhorns in front of me. Besides, I figure Bishop and Abbots would choose the easiest trail to take anyway.'

'Could be you're right. Just take care, but if you have to kill them I'll understand. It's a long way to haul a couple of desperadoes all the way back here from Kansas.'

'Don't worry, Sheriff. I'll fetch them

back to stand trial.'

'Good luck, Carlos.' Henry stepped aside. The new deputy nudged the big sorrel forward and, packhorse in tow, rode out of the town of Big Springs.

He had figured the two fugitives, Bishop and Abbots, would take the easiest route to Abilene. That was, to travel where there were towns on the way; both had grown used to an easy life.

There weren't all that many towns between Texas and Kansas, so he would start his search for them in the dusty little town of Lubbock in the panhandle, the first place he was sure they'd head for. From there he'd go to Amarillo, about a hundred miles further north. From Amarillo they would have made their run along the old Chisholm cattle trail.

That would give them about a 400-mile, straight run, more or less, north to Abilene once they crossed the Red River. It would also put them in Comanche country and they would want to be real careful, but there was no other way that was shorter. Besides, they would be thinking they would be pretty safe being all that distance from Big Springs and their crimes, so perhaps they figured the quicker, more dangerous trip through hostile land to be worth it.

The trail to Kansas was going to be a long one but Carlos had all the time in the world. It really didn't matter how long it took, even if hell itself froze over while he looked for them, he was still going to hunt them down.

He just hoped his guess was right, and that they hadn't headed south for the border: surely they would go north to meet the men who had hired them, maybe to get paid off? Only time would tell.

He reached the junction that split the trail into town about ten minutes after leaving Big Springs and took the left-hand trail that led north towards the town of Lubbock. The right hand trail was hardly ever used any more and went off for another four or five miles before turning and coming back on to itself about ten miles from Lubbock.

It's strange how the fates play with a man's life, he thought as he slowly rode. One day, not far back, he'd had everything to live for. A good woman, a ranch and land that he was building into something; dreams of a future, perhaps some day they would have had kids. Now, in the blink of an eye it had all gone.

Dreams of a happy future had now been replaced by dreams of revenge and death. Clarence Dunsford had been right after all. This land was a killer, it bred killers, it seemed that that was all there was: to kill or be killed. Would it ever stop? He knew it would only stop for him when he had killed those responsible for the death of his family, or was himself killed.

In his reflective mood he nearly missed seeing the rider miles ahead, forking his mount hard and heading across country. The dust cloud billowed out behind him like a vaporous yellow cape.

The rider was too far away to be more than a tiny dot and very soon he vanished out of sight. From the direction he was riding Carlos didn't perceive him as a potential enemy; perhaps just a cowboy heading for Lubbock and a night on the town. He thought no more about him and continued riding on, a broken man with no more to lose, lost in his broken dreams.

The afternoon wore on and he knew he would soon need to find a place to make camp for the night. Up ahead was a small stand of juniper and old pine trees which promised a stream of cool water. It would be an ideal spot to camp.

The shot, when it came, ploughed through the crown of his Stetson, sending it flying. Instantly, without thinking, he reacted by throwing himself sideways from the saddle opposite to the side from where the shot had come.

Damn! This was becoming a habit: being shot at.

The ground was open except for a few boulders and he knew he was a sitting duck. The horses milled around for a few vital moments, allowing him to use an old Apache trick.

Quickly picking out the nearest, biggest rock, one that was about the size of a man's torso, he ran to it and dropped lengthways behind. Unless the hidden gunman was high up in one of the trees, which was doubtful, he would find it almost impossible to put a slug into his intended victim.

Now Carlos could last it out till nightfall, another hour away maybe, and then he could seek out his assailant in the dark. That would make the odds a damn sight more even. The would-be assassin must have been thinking along the same lines, not fancying taking his chances with his intended victim in the dark, for a few minutes later the sound of drumming horse's hoofs could be heard as the would-be killer made his escape.

Carlos gave him a few minutes to get

clear, then went over to where he had laid his ambush. He could plainly see where whoever it had been had crushed down the grass as he lay in the spot he had picked out from which to kill the young cowboy.

Scouting around a bit more he suddenly picked out a very clear hoof-print. There could be no doubt whatsoever: there, in the soft ground, was the same print he had seen in his yard. He sat on a stump and tried to get things clear in his mind. There were only two people who knew he was heading to Kansas: the sheriff and Lars Beauchamp.

Now he hadn't noticed Henry's horse, nor for that matter had he noticed Beauchamp's; either man could be the ambusher but his money was on the banker.

Beauchamp! Of course, it had to be him, considering his downright, obstinate refusal to divulge the names of the killer consortium and his statement about Indians. And he knew Carlos carried $80,000.

It all added up, but he only had that one piece of evidence: the cracked horseshoe; little enough to charge a man of Beauchamp's standing in the town.

But then another thought occurred. Surely Beauchamp wouldn't have done all these grisly things himself. For one thing he was a poor specimen of manhood, so that would suggest that he had hired someone, someone other than Boscombe, Abbots and Bishop. Somebody who had not ridden with them after Dunsford's womenfolk.

Suddenly the need to get Bishop and Abbots became the most important thing in his life, to bring them back to Big Springs and have them talk. He doubted his would-be killer would come back and try again, so after gathering up the horses and finding his bullet-holed hat, he made camp for the night.

After seeing to the needs of the horses he made himself a dry camp, not wanting to take the extra risk that a fire would expose him to.

In the morning, bright and early, he saddled up and took the trail again.

Eventually he reached the town of Lubbock. After asking around in the lower parts of town and throwing around a few dollars in the right places he learned that two men answering the description of the men he sought had passed through on their way north about three weeks earlier.

One of them had seemed well-heeled and was forever flashing large sums of money around. That certainly sounded like Abbots: he was always a flashy bastard.

So they had a very good start on him, but he wasn't worried.

The longer they remained unpunished for what they had done back in Texas the more relaxed and at ease they would feel. They thought Carlos to be dead, so he wouldn't even enter their thoughts, unless . . .

Someone had tried to kill him to stop

him getting to Abilene and had failed. He would have to try again but they would know that by now Carlos would be doubly vigilant and that would make it harder, maybe fatal for him to try again.

Then the answer was obvious. Telegraph! That was all they had to do. Send a wire from Big Springs and the others would be watching for him in Abilene. There could be any number of them and he wouldn't know. But why hadn't the bushwhacker just done that instead of trying the dangerous ploy of ambush, knowing the tables could have just as easily turned on the bushwhacker? The answer seemed to be simple enough. The back-shooter must have thought he could easily do the job himself. As that plan had failed he'd report back to the banker, who would now have to warn the others in Kansas.

However, the only two who knew what he looked like were Bishop and Abbots. If he could find them quickly enough and get away with them he could still pull it off. He had nothing to lose, so that made him easy, not caring too much for the risks.

On the other hand he wasn't about to go charging into Abilene like a Texas longhorn bull with its tail on fire; but the hate he felt for these men and what they had done had erased any fear he might have felt for his own skin.

Of course, now he must assume that the consortium, whoever they were, would be warned of his coming and the reasons for it, and would be watching and waiting for him, ready to kill him the moment he arrived in Abilene.

He guessed they would be looking for him to come into Abilene from the south, from the direction of Big Springs, along the old Chisholm Trail. However, if he were to swing due east for a few extra miles, then head north, he would, eventually, pick up the Smoky Hill Trail and come into the town from the north-east. Maybe that was the only break he was going to get, but maybe it was the only one he needed.

The days became indistinguishable, riding all day, camping at night, mostly dry camps, not seeing another soul. One day just rolled into another until he lost all concept of time, but he reckoned that he must have been on the trail for at least three or four weeks.

The harsh, dry Texas country he'd been riding through for so long gradually began to give way to more and more grass and even some undulating hills. He was able to bring down a pronghorn antelope, risking a shot for the sweet flesh that would be a welcome change from bacon, beef jerky, hardtack and Johnny-cakes.

As the surroundings began to change he realized he was getting closer to the northern boundary of Texas and would soon be entering into the greener countryside of Kansas. Now he must travel more carefully, for whoever he met on the trail from now on, he would have to consider an enemy. Also the threat of the Comanche was now very real.

13

It sure made a fella aware of his surroundings. He even became aware of the high, musical notes of a singing fieldlark, and realized just how intent on his goal he had been over the last few weeks. The birds and wildlife had been around him, of course, throughout the long journey, he just hadn't consciously noticed them.

He saw no sign of the dreaded Comanche, perhaps they had already gone to their winter grounds in Comancheria, or they were engaged elsewhere, perhaps fighting running skirmishes with the army along the border, but whatever the reason, Carlos counted it as lucky.

He was making a good fifteen miles a day without being too hard on the horses. But he still had a long way to go.

The days, thankfully, were cool and pleasant and if his mind had not been on more bitter things he probably would have enjoyed the trip.

At night, camped out under the stars, his thoughts would return time and time again to what had happened to his life.

The loss of his wife was with him every moment, worse at nights when he tried to sleep. Eventually exhaustion would overtake him and he would fall into a restless fitful sleep, awakening at dawn feeling tired, washed-out and empty.

Each new day he would get up, see to the horses, then eat food he prepared. But he ate with no real enjoyment; it merely provided the strength he needed to carry on.

One morning, when the loneliness of the trip was becoming more than even Carlos thought he could bear, he topped a small rise and there, spread out before him was the town of Abilene. He sat and looked at it for a while, noting its lay-out in his mind. Once satisfied that he had missed nothing he turned and headed off the trail.

There was a knot of trees about five miles away to the east where he could leave the packhorse securely tethered for the day out of sight. He would clean the trail dust off himself and swap clothes, replacing those he had travelled in for those that would see him as just another businessman in Abilene, there to make another beef deal.

He would also need to buy more supplies. It went against the grain but he would have to feed his prisoners on the way back.

An hour later, washed and shaved, using the water from the little stream that fed itself reluctantly into the Mud River running to the east of the town, his long hair slicked back and dressed like a Texas cattle breeder, he mounted up and headed into Abilene.

He would make his purchases, look around at the layout of the town, fixing points he had noticed from the ridge, maybe ask a few questions, then come back here and lie low until nightfall.

He entered the town just as a couple of drunken cowboys decided to end the quarrel they were having with their pistols. Under the cover of their gunplay he was able to slip in barely noticed.

It didn't take long to find the livery stable among the jumble of false-fronted buildings. He needed to rest the sorrel, he might be needing him right quickly.

'Gonna be travelling far?'

'Yeah, heading up to Montana. Heard there's good cattle-grazing land for sale.'

'Well, you Texicans sure know about good grazing land down there in the south-west.' The livery man said this with a wink. Then more seriously he added: 'But you sure as hell know how to grow cattle, I'll give you that. Sure know how to throw your money around too.'

'How so?'

'Couple you Texican boys arrived here 'bout three, four weeks ago and ain't stepped out of the saloon or the whorehouse since they got here.' He cackled a sly old laugh and poked a bony finger into Carlos's ribs.

Carlos laughed along with him but his blood was suddenly racing and his heart began pounding in his chest so loudly he wondered whether the old man could hear it.

'Well, you know, I knew a couple of old pards like that a few years ago, haven't seen them in an age, I wonder . . . ? No, surely not. Say, you don't happen to know their names, do you, old-timer?'

'Sure. Bishop and Abbots, them's the monikers they be usin'. When they first arrived it looked like they'd rode their horses inta the ground like all the Comanche devils from hell had been achasin 'em. Sold 'em a couple of good horses too. They paid in cash, that's why I knows them so well. In fact that's their horses over there in that stall.

Hardly ever take 'em out, like I said; too busy either over to the saloon or hanging out at Annie's.'

'What time you close up shop here, old-timer?' Carlos pulled a twenty-dollar bill out of his pocket and innocently dangled it in front of the liveryman.

''Bout six o'clock.' The old-timer's eyes never left the twenty.

'How about before you leave tonight you saddle up those two horses and leave your side door open?'

For the first time the old hostler looked closer at the young man standing there in the stable's gloom. Suddenly he saw the tin star under his jacket.

'Montana, eh?'

Carlos shrugged. 'How about it?'

'What they wanted for?

'Murder.'

'Well, I never held much for no murderers. Put your money away, son. I'll do as you ask.'

'Thanks. Where do you think I'll find

them about ten o'clock tonight?'

'That Abbots, he's sweet on one of Annie's girls, you'll prob'ly find them there. That's her place just opposite the general store, red building. Don't worry about your horse, I'll see to him.'

The general store was the next stop and he stocked up on what he would need for the trip back. On the way up here he had been able to hunt, adding pronghorn antelope and the odd jack rabbit to supplement his menu. He knew he wouldn't be able to do that going back, so he made sure he bought enough. When the clerk was finished adding it all up he gave Carlos a funny look.

'You either travelling all the way to California or you're a man with a big appetite.'

'Well, I hate to travel on an empty stomach, besides I might be able to use it to trade my way out of trouble if I meet any Comanches.'

'Last I heard the soldiers from Fort Worth were out hunting them. Seems

Quanah Parker's gone on the warpath again.'

'That so?'

He reflected on what the clerk had said on his way back to where he'd left the other horse, always keeping an eye out on his back trail.

It seemed that he was the only person in Kansas who was out and about at this time of the day, which suited him fine.

14

It was dark when he reached the outskirts of Abilene and tethered the horses outside the livery stable. He'd entered again from the old Smoky Hill Trail, hoping that if they were looking for him they had their eyes pointed in the other direction.

The Mud River sparkled in the moonlight as he tied the horses behind the livery stable and crept through the shadows to try the door. True to his word the owner had left it unlocked.

A piano could be heard tinkling away down Texas Street, the main street of Abilene, probably coming from the saloon called the Drover's Cottage, the establishment where all the cattle buyers and drovers met and thousands of dollars' worth of business was set up. It was more than likely the place to meet the two he sought as well as those who made up the consortium.

He walked down the boardwalk on the opposite side to the saloon, his moccasined feet making no noise, and keeping as much in the shadows as he could until he reached the garish, red-painted building that was the town brothel. That, perhaps, might be the easiest place to begin.

As he neared the building he heard the front door open and a woman laugh as a man stepped out into the night. Her loud brazen voice followed him.

'See you soon, Fes honey.'

He froze where he stood; the man who had just come outside stood under a lantern that threw out a red light, adding to the already hellish exterior of the whorehouse, and built himself a smoke. He struck a match on the side of his boot, lighted the smoke and inhaled.

He had his back to Carlos, who just kept standing there in the shadows, waiting for him to finish.

As he took the last drag and prepared

to flip the butt away, Carlos stepped quietly up behind him and clamped his left hand over the startled man's mouth.

'If you make a wrong move, Bishop, I'll slice your kidneys in half.' The whispered voice in his ear sent Bishop rigid with fear and he slowly nodded his head in understanding.

'Step back here into the shadows.'

Bishop was pulled backwards into an alley at the side.

'OK, where's Abbots?'

'Christ, man, you gave me a fright, sneaking up like th — '

Without warning, as quick as lightning, Carlos's knife hand struck out and the sharp blade was at Bishop's throat, the point already drawing a bubble of blood. Carlos took the frightened man's pistol and put it in the waistband of his pants. 'I asked you a question,' he said.

Bishop looked at his attacker with frightened eyes. That look turned into one of horror as he recognized the man who held the knife.

'Christ, we thought you was dead.'

The knife pressed harder.

'He's in there, with his woman.'

'How long's he gonna be?'

'We was just leaving.'

'When he comes out you call him over here. If you try to be clever, Fes, I'll gut you like a pig.' Carlos pushed the knife point a little deeper into Bishop's neck. This time the little bubble became a tiny river.

Bishop caught Carlos's drift.

'C'mon, Clem. It's damned cold out here.'

Clem Abbots stepped out into the night, squinting into the darkness, looking for his pard. He heard the sound as Carlos cocked his pistol.

'What you do in the next few seconds decides whether or not I gut shoot you, Abbots.'

Abbots slowly raised his hands and Carlos quickly stepped forward and relieved him also of his six-shooter. 'Now we're going to go grab your horses, then we're going for a little ride. Move!'

It didn't take long to get them mounted up and heading out of town the way he'd come in. He kept them moving until they were well clear of Abilene, then he called a halt.

He made Abbots tie Bishop's hands together, then his feet under his horse's belly.

When Abbots had done this, Carlos did the same to him. When he was well satisfied that the knots were tight and would hold he quickly tied the lead reins of the packhorse to Abbots's saddle, wanting to put as much distance as possible between them and the town by morning.

They travelled easily through the darkness; the moon was enough to light the way and come morning Carlos had found a small grove of trees for shelter. Untying their feet he ordered the two men to dismount. When they were on the ground looking at him expectantly, probably wondering when he was going to shoot them, he began to talk to them.

'This is the way it's going to be. I'm going to take you both back to Big Springs to stand trial for murder. Now, you can either hang by yourselves or tell me who the members of this consortium are who put you all up to it.'

They traded looks with each other before Abbots spoke.

'What the hell you talking about, Williams? What damned consortium?'

'Don't know nothin 'bout no consortium, it was just La — '

Abbots landed a vicious kick into Bishop's leg, causing him to howl and dodge away.

'Shut yer mouth, yer danged fool.'

Bishop sat down heavily on a half-rotted stump and almost immediately jumped to his feet with a yelp. 'Christ! I've been bitten.' The angry sound of a rattler could be clearly heard.

Carlos moved cautiously closer to Bishop, expecting some trick. He pointed the pistol at Abbots. 'See what's ailing him.'

Abbot went to Bishop and tried to stop him jumping about, but with his own hands still tied behind him it was mighty awkward. If Bishop had been bitten then the more he moved around the faster the venom would travel through his body.

Carlos had no other choice.

'Get over here, Abbots.'

When he came over Carlos tied his hands to a twisted branch of a fallen tree. If he wanted to run he would have to take the whole damn tree with him. Then quickly he went over to Bishop and laid the pistol barrel across his head. Down he went, out cold. At least he had stopped jumping around.

He looked first at Bishop's hands. Sure enough there they were already beginning to puff up and swell; two tell-tale puncture marks were slowly weeping blood and poison on the side of his left palm.

Carlos moved behind the stump Bishop had unwisely chosen to sit upon without looking first and there was the snake; it was a Western diamondback, his tail still raised and his body in the distinctive S-shaped defensive position.

With a quick, well-aimed backward flick, Carlos cut the snake's head off before it could do any more damage.

But for Bishop the damage had already been done. It could be clearly seen by the other two men that he was beginning to go into shock as the poison quickly worked its way through his body. As he lay on the ground his breathing was becoming laboured, he was beginning to sweat profusely; his skin colour was beginning to change also, his face becoming pale and ashen.

It took about three hours for him to die. In all that time Carlos sat and watched their back trail, making sure that no one who came along was alerted to the groaning of the dying man. All that time he kept Abbots tied to the tree.

'By God, Williams, you just gonna let him die?'

Carlos ignored him. He knew there was nothing he or anyone else could do to save Bishop.

When at last Bishop lay still Carlos checked him to make sure he was dead, then when he was certain he went over and untied Abbots from the tree.

'Mount up, we'll move some place else.'

'You gonna bury him, Williams?'

'You mean like he buried my wife and her brother, Abbots? What do you think? Do you want his jacket? It gets cold on the trail at night.'

'I ain't wearin no dead man's clothes.'

'Suit yourself.'

'You're a cold son of a bitch, Williams.'

'If you want to see just how cold I can be, put a foot wrong. Just give me a reason — any reason — to blast you.'

'No! I won't give you that satisfaction, you bastard. You'll get no trouble from me. It's a long way back though; anything might happen.' Then he added thoughtfully. 'But I'm quite happy to take my chances with the sheriff.'

'Probably another bad choice, Abbots. He wants to see you hang as much as I do.'

'Yeah? Well, I guess we'll have to see about that.' He sounded very confident for a man heading back to get his neck stretched. But Carlos didn't push it. After tying Abbots securely to his horse and leading Bishop's, they headed out.

15

On the morning of the fifth day out of Abilene Carlos cut fresh Indian sign. Comanches!

There were about five of them, probably a hunting party.

He decided that their safest way back now would be to travel at night and hole up during the day, which was what they were doing at the moment after having a cold meal of beef jerky and hardtack washed down with tepid water from their canteens. It would be madness even to think of a cooking-fire.

As a man who was half-Apache Carlos was under no illusions as to what would be his fate should he fall into the hands of the Comanches. The Apache and Comanche had been at each other's throats for hundreds of bitter years, honing their skills at torture and death, raiding each other's villages, raping, killing and taking prisoners long before the white man even dreamed of crossing the Atlantic to colonize this vast land.

If they should meet up in the near future then Carlos would save one bullet for himself. Abbots could sample their hospitality, he cared not.

Abbots sensed the tenseness in his captor and guessed what it was he was fretting about.

'Comanches?'

Carlos said nothing.

'For God's sake, Williams, what if they find us? You'll have to give me a gun.'

'Now that's never going to happen, Abbots, and you know it.'

'What if they kill you? What will happen to me?'

'You have an imagination, you bastard. Use it. All the things you thought the Apaches capable of, well double that and you're just starting to get warm.'

Suddenly Carlos saw an opportunity. 'Tell you what, Abbots. Those Comanches find us and I'll give you a gun providing you give me some information now.'

Abbots looked a little doubtful as he contemplated the offer.

'You promise, Williams? You've always been noted for keeping your word, 'breed or not.'

'Yeah, I promise.'

'All Harvey wanted to do was kill you. He wanted nothing else, he didn't want your land because he knew the Indians, your kin, would never let him keep it. He felt his whole life that you were superior to him. Everything you did worked out well. He was jealous, pure and simple. When you bust his head that day, well, that was the final straw. I guess he went sorta crazy after that.'

'What about the attack on my home? The murder of my wife, and her brother?'

'Yes, Harvey rode with us that night but by then we'd been approached by . . . let's say . . . some other interested parties who wanted your land, Claiborne's and Dunsford's. If it makes you feel any better we didn't know there was anyone at your place that night. We were told they had all gone to some big powwow up in the mountains and all we had to do was make it look like the work of Indians.'

'No, Abbots, it doesn't make me feel any better. You must have got that telegram from Big Springs warning you I was coming. How come you allowed yourselves to get caught so easy?'

'Yeah, but when you took so long getting to Abilene we figured the hostiles got you.'

'Who was it sent that wire, Abbots? Was it Beauchamp?'

Suddenly Abbots stopped talking, becoming thoughtful for a few minutes, perhaps realizing how close he was to dying right then. 'I have a deal of my own, Williams. I'm not going to tell you any more until we get closer to Big Springs and out of Injun country. If I tell you everything I know right off what's to stop you putting a bullet in me and saying the Injuns got me or I got shot trying to escape?'

Well, he had a point, Carlos had to admit; that very thought was right now fighting for dominance in his mind. But he could see that through fear for his skin Abbots had made up his mind and, rather than getting physical with him and making him talk, which Carlos had no intention of doing, he decided instead to ponder on what he had already been told.

But through the twist and turns of it all he began to realize that this idea of a consortium from Kansas was beginning to stink higher than a polecat three days dead. He tried to remember who it was who had mentioned the idea of a consortium.

The sheriff! Could *he* have been wrong and if so who had fed that idea to him in the first place?

Again Beauchamp's name sprang to mind.

And so it was! The closer they came to Big Springs, the more Abbots talked. By the time they hit the main street of Big Springs, both tired and trail-dirty,

Carlos had all the information he needed to see Abbots hang, except the name of the person or persons who had put them up to their mission of killing the major landowners in the county, namely, Dunsford, Claiborne and Williams himself.

A sizeable crowd began to grow as word of their arrival spread and by the time they fetched up outside the sheriff's office there were about thirty townsfolk waiting there, all talking at once.

Henry Dodds stepped out on to the boardwalk, a grin the size of the Colorado River on his face.

'Well, Carlos, congratulations. Some folks here,' he nodded towards the crowd which had now grown quiet, 'thought you'd never make it, but I never doubted you for an instant. Now let's get him inside.'

With Abbots safely behind bars at last, Carlos allowed himself to relax a little. What he needed was a bath, a change of clothes and some sleep.

He told the sheriff everything Abbots had told him on the trail, omitting nothing. 'Except who it was that put them up to it. He knows but he isn't saying.'

'Well, you just leave that to me, son, and you get off and get some rest. Oh, by the way, you won't be needing that star any more. You've done the job. Pity about Bishop but that's how it goes.'

Carlos took the weary horses to the livery stable. 'Clarry, give them a good rub-down and feed them well. They've earned it.'

It was then that he noticed the fresh print in the dust of the floor. It was unmistakable, that split in the shoe on the right front foot.

'Clarry, the horse that made those prints: who does it belong to?'

The old man gazed down at where he pointed, squinting feeble eyes at the ground.

'Shucks, son, that's Sheriff Dodds's horse, been out early this morning and only just got back — just before you rode in with that Abbots fella.'

Clarry's words hit Carlos with the force of a physical body blow. Had he been mistaken, thinking all this time that Beauchamp was behind it when all along it was Henry?

There was obviously some mistake. He had known Henry Dodds for most of his life and as far as he could recollect Dodds had always been the sheriff here in Big Springs and was well liked and respected.

However, at that very moment young Pete Munny came running into the stable. He was panting and out of breath; they waited for him to suck in some air.

'Mr Williams, I saw you come in here with the horses and came over to warn you.'

'Warn me about what, Pete?'

'Sheriff Dodds's getting some townsfolk together to arrest you.'

The room suddenly seemed to spin. Carlos couldn't believe his ears. 'On what charge?'

'The murder of Fes Bishop. He said you gunned him down in cold blood while his hands were tied back there on the trail. Clem Abbots is an eyewitness and between them they're sure getting the folks riled up, some are even talking of a lynchin'.'

Carlos turned, looking for Clarry Benson, another man he'd known all his life. He'd disappeared but then he stepped out of the shadows of the stable, leading a big chestnut gelding.

'Your horses are plumb done in, Carlos. Put your gear on this one. He's fresh.'

It was quickly done and Carlos, now a wanted man, sprang up on the chestnut's back. 'I owe you both; I won't forget your help.' Then, with a slap of the reins across the horse's broad neck he was thundering out of the town towards Apache territory. He heard angry shouting and a couple of slugs buzzed past his ears but there was no pursuit.

16

He rode hard, putting distance between himself and the town. Everything had changed in the space of just over an hour. It must have been Henry who had tried to bushwhack him when he left Big Springs to go after Bishop and Abbots. Having missed killing him he'd returned to town and sent a message to Abilene in an attempt to warn the two there that Carlos was on his way to arrest them.

It all fitted. Henry's story of a consortium of buyers from Kansas was just that: a story invented for the purpose of steering attention away from himself.

No wonder Abbots had been so sure of himself, so confident that he told everything except that it was Dodds all along who was the mastermind. He didn't tell Carlos that, obviously, because he needed Dodds for protection and to see he never went to trial.

He stopped and rested the horse while at the same time checking the trail behind. It all seemed empty as far as he could see, and there were no dust clouds sent up by a following posse. He began to wonder why he hadn't been pursued. Maybe they could have caught up with him before he reached safety with his mother's people, or maybe Henry had wanted him to escape.

Now he was nothing more than a murdering half-breed renegade on the run from the white man's justice, a target to be shot first and questioned later. It would be conveniently forgotten that he was the son of Andrew Williams, one of the men who had helped carve out Big Springs and had supported the fledgling town from its very beginning. After Henry was through talking him down, all they would see was a killer in need of hanging.

He had no doubt that some in the town would support him: men like

Clarry and Pete and even Nora Harding, but for how long?

He would not be around to proclaim his innocence, nor that of the Apaches. How could he possibly accuse Henry Dodds with Abbots backing every word the sheriff said?

Yes, Henry Dodds had worked everything out perfectly.

But there was one thing.

In all of this his wife had still been killed along with Nairn. Accident or not, somebody was responsible and it looked as though that was down to Henry, and perhaps Beauchamp also, for he began to believe the pair of them were in it together. Otherwise, surely Beauchamp would have denied all knowledge of a consortium. Instead, he'd played right along.

The hot, arid land began to change as he rode closer to the mountains. Chaparral and sage began to give way to struggling mesquite and creosote bushes.

Carlos must try to come up with a

way to bring these men to justice without spilling any more Apache blood or any innocent white blood.

That was going to be hard because unless he could persuade Nadie's father, Owl Talker, to do otherwise, he would take to the war path and many whites would die, along with a whole lot of good Apaches.

He eventually reached the foothills and the broken desert gave way to endless canyons; canyons that had caught out many an unwary traveller in their mazes. However, Carlos knew this land well and the canyon he chose to disappear into seemed like just a narrow crack in the rock wall. The canyon he entered was indeed narrow, barely wide enough for the horse, and occasionally Carlos would scrape his feet on the walls. The floor was littered with boulders of various sizes, making the gelding step carefully.

The walls were weather-tested, rising sheer some eighty feet or more and being topped with broken, sawtooth ridges.

Another hour's riding and he saw the

first Indian sign: a scuffed moccasin print on a dust-covered rock. He knew they were watching him.

He took the gelding up a steep slope that was hard work on the horse. Its haunches sank into the soft scree but it pumped and pushed with powerful back legs and soon they were at the top.

And found the Apaches waiting.

'The old one wants to talk with you, little brother.'

'That is good, big brother, for I must speak with him also.'

'There is talk that the whites intend to fight us for things we haven't done. But if they want such a fight then they should have it.'

Carlos held his peace, wondering how many other young bucks felt the same way as Two Eagle Claw. He also wondered if Owl Talker was strong enough to keep them from the path that led to bloodshed.

Owl Talker stood outside his wickiup and watched the riders approach. 'It is good to see you alive, my son. I thank the gods for watching over you.'

'Thank you, Father, for your concern.'

'Did you achieve what you set out to do?'

Carlos told him what had happened since the last time he had seen Owl Talker, when he had ridden out on the vengeance trail.

'It seems there is no end to the treachery of the white man.'

'It is as you say, Father.'

'What now, my son? Have you plans or do I rise up with my warriors and burn Big Springs to the ground and kill every white man in the territory?'

'Father, I have a plan but I cannot do it alone, I need your help.'

'Very well, come inside. We will smoke and talk.' He turned to his wife Anita. 'We will drink coffee, strong, sweet and hot.'

Carlos followed him into his lodge.

After Owl Talker had lit one of the evil-smelling Mexican cigarillos, favoured by the Apache and harsh enough to make eyes water in the confines of a wickiup, the coffee arrived. They held the steaming-hot cups of thick, sweet coffee in their hands and savoured the rich, fragrant aroma. Neither of them wanted to break the pleasant moment with cold, grim reality.

But it had to be done. Owl Talker spoke first.

'What of your plan?'

'The banker, Beauchamp: we must capture him and bring him here. He must be frightened into telling us everything he knows, but at the same time we must also capture and bring in Judge Whittiker. Each must not know of the other's presence. We will get the banker to talk while the judge listens then . . . '

As they discussed the plan it grew dark. Anita stepped into the wickiup and brought them two plates of piping hot venison stew. Carlos, who hadn't had time to eat since fleeing the town, realized just how tired and hungry he was.

After the meal was finished Carlos yawned.

'You can sleep in the wickiup of my son; now it is yours.'

'Thank you, Father. I am very tired.'

'Then go and rest; you will need all your strength to make your plan succeed.'

He stood up. 'Goodnight, Father, sleep well.'

'As with you my son.'

The next morning he was up early, feeling refreshed and hungry. Leosanni suddenly appeared at the flap of the doorway carrying a bundle.

'Good morning,' she greeted him.

She put the bundle down. 'Father told me to give you these Indian clothes. He would like to see you dressed decently for once.' He liked her attempt at humour.

He picked up the bundle she had brought to him. It consisted of fresh, Apache clothes. Soon he was dressed in loose-fitting white cotton trousers, over which he donned a long red breech-clout. A faded calico shirt was topped by leather, sleeveless jerkin. On his feet, he placed the comfortably soft and pliant boot moccasins. He slipped the cloth headband around his forehead and instantly he was every bit an Apache.

17

Night approached slowly and they prepared themselves for what lay ahead. Eight of them would sneak into the town of Big Springs and make their play in the hours just before first light. This was the Apache way, attacking just before dawn when there was barely enough light to see a hundred yards ahead.

The main street with the livery stable and bakehouse, next to Nora Harding's general store and the sheriff's office, ran north to south. They rode in this direction and quietly passed the grey stone frontage of the Big Spring's bank, past Toby Granger's lumber yard, then the group split up.

Three of them, led by Two Eagles Claw, turned west into Grace Street where they headed for the neat little clapboard house that belonged to Lars Beauchamp.

Carlos carried on a little further, then turned south into Commerce Street where he sought the home of Judge Wallace Whittiker. As he drew near his goal he knew he had better get this plan one hundred per cent right because he was just about to kidnap a federal-appointed judge and that alone was enough to put a price on his head. That was, if Henry Dodds hadn't already done so.

The judge was mightily put out to say the least. After entering his house with ease they had found him working in his study, still dressed in his everyday clothes.

'I hope you know what you're doing, Carlos. You could and probably will hang for this.'

'That's a risk I'll have to take, Judge. Believe me if I thought there was another way, an easier way, I would do it but I can't think of one. Not one that wouldn't get me shot on sight.'

'The sheriff has a warrant out for your arrest, Carlos. Two thousand dollars dead or alive. And he's sending away to Fort Worth for soldiers to track down the guilty Apaches.'

'Judge, we'd better get moving and you need to grab a jacket; it gets cold up in the mountains.'

Without any problems arising, they got back to the village hours later and took the judge to a clean wickiup that had been newly built for his stay.

An Apache wickiup was quite an easy affair to make. A circular ring of cottonwood or mesquite poles, longer than the height of a tall man were tied together at the top and each pole was forced into the ground about a yard apart. Once spread and set in place they were interlocked with twigs and branches and bound with yucca fibre rope. This was then covered with brush and bear grass, or sometimes army canvas.

They wanted the judge to be as comfortable as possible, so they had also placed soft robes of thick bearskin for him to rest on.

However, the lodge set up for Beauchamp was an old storehouse, rat infested and crawling with insect life. The interior was kept dark and the skeletal heads of dead animals festooned the walls and peered menacingly down on any occupant.

The new wickiup had been placed and built in such a manner as to be right alongside the other, older one. Any one talking there could be overheard with very little difficulty.

Carlos and the men with him had done nothing to disguise themselves, even leaving their faces unpainted. They had done all in their power to treat Judge Whittiker in as friendly and unthreatening a manner as possible.

For Lars Beauchamp, however, it had been the exact opposite.

He lived alone, a man not taken greatly with women since his own wife had died in childbirth eighteen years ago, along with the baby. Ever since then he had turned all his energies inward and had dedicated the rest of his life to building up his bank and his own personal wealth.

Lars had gone to bed early, hoping to arise just as early in the morning. There were deeds and papers to sign that would finalize the sale of Dunsford's spread, then the widow was leaving, going back to England. He would have been a happy man if it were not for the fact that that blasted half-breed Williams was still on the loose. Still, he had no difficulty dropping off to sleep.

Several hours later he awoke to see a painted-faced demon from hell glaring down at him, a huge, bone-handled hunting knife held inches from his face. Before he could scream a hand clamped tightly against his mouth and a whispered warning to be quiet was uttered. Three other demons stood around his bed, their faces painted in grotesque patterns in horrid red-and-black ochre that chilled the banker's heart and set his teeth chattering.

He heard words spoken in some diabolically infernal language as he was pulled roughly from his bed. A blanket was thrown across his shoulders and he was led outside and mounted on a horse; a gag was tied securely round his mouth.

Within minutes he was leaving the warmth of his bed behind him and, for all he knew, was riding into the very bowels of hell with these painted sons of Satan.

Two Eagles Claw rode into the village about an hour after Carlos. His journey had been slowed by the woeful lack of Beauchamp's riding skills. When they lifted him from the saddle he collapsed on to his knees, wobbly and frightened almost to death.

Carlos walked over to where the terrified banker knelt and looked down at this man who, he suspected, had helped to bring such misery into his life and the lives of so many others. 'Get up, Beauchamp.'

The banker looked up, surprise and confusion rippled over his face, then a look of recognition followed immediately by a look of fear.

'Carlos.'

'Get up.' Rifle barrels poked him in the back, forcing him to his feet. With a terrified whimper he followed his captor into the old wickiup prepared for him. Once they were inside Carlos turned to him. Now was the time to begin putting together the rest of his plan.

'Do you have any idea how much pain the Apaches can inflict on a man and still keep him alive?'

'Carlos, for God's sake help me.'

'Help you, Beauchamp! Now why would I want to do that? Here you are, the man responsible for the death of my wife, her brother, Clarence Dunsford and Jeb Claiborne. You probably killed Harvey Boscombe as well but that don't matter none to me. Saved me doing it.'

'It wasn't me who did the killings, Carlos, you must believe that. There — there were others involved.'

'Well, if you value keeping hold of your skin, Lars, now's the time to tell all.'

The banker had been a hard case

when it came to enforcing foreclosures on poverty-stricken families, mostly women bereft of husbands. His heart was a rock when he dealt with such people and he considered himself a true *hombre*. But right now all he could think about was saving his skin. Trembling, he began to talk.

'When the Comancheros took Dunsford's women and you all trailed off after them, Henry Dodds came to see me and asked if I'd thought about what would happen if you all got yourselves killed.'

Once he'd started talking his fear for his life kept him at it.

'At first I couldn't see what he was driving at and explained that your land was in your name and Dunsford's and Claiborne's was in theirs, and none of you had wills. This would exclude the women being able to claim title so the land would go up for auction. Henry suggested a way to avoid that and allow us to buy up both ranches at next to nothing.'

Suddenly it fell into place. 'The consortium?'

'Yes. If we invented a false group of buyers already there with the cash there would be no need of a public auction. It seemed like the biggest obstacle to the plan would be you. When Harvey Boscombe rode into town after the rescue and told everybody that you had been killed in a rock fall, well that simplified everything.'

'You said there were others involved, apart from the sheriff. Who were they?'

'There was only one other, Nora Harding.'

'Nora Harding!' In spite of himself he couldn't stop from showing his surprise.

'Yes. She and Henry Dodds have been an item for some time now.'

Suddenly Carlos needed air. He told the two Apache guards to watch Beauchamp carefully, then stepped out into the night.

His thoughts were reeling with what he'd just been told.

It was several minutes before he felt up to entering the other wickiup where Judge Whittiker was.

'Did you catch all that, Judge?' The look on the judge's face told him he had. 'Do you see why I brought you here? How could I ever have proved any of this? My word against the sheriff's, with Nora Harding backing up anything he said, and Beauchamp, not to mention Abbots. I'm just a half-breed renegade Apache, with a price on his head for a murder I didn't commit. Who would listen to me?'

'I don't believe what I heard, Carlos. I have known these people for years, they are, were good people.' The judge was as shocked as Carlos.

'Greed can make folks do strange things, Judge, and if they get away with it they will be very wealthy.'

'They mustn't get away with it, Carlos; they must be brought to justice and hanged. They have cost too many people their lives. There is no place on God's good earth for a law officer turn crooked. Dodds will be hunted down.'

Carlos thought deeply for a few moments. 'Well, Judge, I think that by now he will know that both you and Beauchamp are missing. He may have turned renegade, but Henry Dodds is no fool. If he even suspects that I am behind your disappearance he will put two and two together and see that it's all up for him; he'll make a run for it.'

'We must get back to town and stop him. However, there is one other thing, Carlos.'

'What is it, Judge?'

'You must not let the Apaches here kill Beauchamp. We must take him back to stand trial.'

'Owl Talker lost a daughter and a son because of Beauchamp and the others; they don't have the others but they do have Beauchamp.'

'Carlos, if the sheriff has taken the owl-hoot trail then someone in authority must go after him and bring him back. I want that person to be you as a duly appointed marshal, but I can't swear you in if you don't take Beauchamp back to town alive.'

Suddenly Carlos was torn between his desire to see Beauchamp die at the hands of Talking Owl and doing what Judge Whittiker wanted; saving Beauchamp's life even though he didn't deserve it ate away at him.

'Carlos, it's the right thing to do. Otherwise you're just like them.'

He thought of Nadie. What would she have him do? But he knew the answer to that already.

'Stay here, Judge. I'll go and talk with them.'

At first some of the younger bucks were angry; they'd been looking forward to hearing this murderer scream and beg for mercy. Almost all of them had been friends of Nairn. But it was Owl Talker who prevailed.

'What our brother says is true; let this wicked man find justice at the end of the white man's rope. For too long the Apache has been seen as a bloodthirsty savage in the eyes of the whites. This is now a chance to show them that we are a people capable of restraint. If we kill this man the soldiers will ride against us, and while I do not fear them I fear the results of such fighting. Our braves will die and we cannot replace them. Soldiers too, will die but more and more of them will come, for their replacements are easily found.'

Owl Talker had always been seen as being a wise and good leader, so they listened to him now. Beauchamp was brought out into the sunshine, blinking in its harsh glare. Roughly he was lifted and placed once again in the saddle.

Judge Whittiker was also escorted out and soon he too was mounted.

Something went out of Beauchamp the instant he saw the judge and he cast his eyes to the ground.

Owl Talker looked at the dejected white man with disgust, then turned to Carlos. 'I will send Two Eagles Claw with you, he will watch for you from the rise above the town. If anything happens to you then we will attack the town and destroy everyone and everything in it.'

'It is as you say, Father.' Carlos climbed once again on to the gelding's broad back and they began to make their way towards the waiting town of Big Springs and whatever lay in store.

However, before they rode off Judge Whittiker asked Carlos to raise his right hand.

When he had done so the judge looked him squarely in the face. 'Do you, Carlos Williams, swear to uphold the laws of the territory of Texas and of this county to the best of your ability?'

The young cowboy looked back at him, equally serious. 'I do.'

'Now everything is legal, Carlos,' the judge stated happily. 'When we get back to town I will give you a marshal's badge. Wear it with pride.'

18

Two Eagles Claw dropped behind them to take up his vigil once they reached the little knoll that overlooked the northern approach to the town. The sun was getting high overhead when they reached its outskirts. It seemed unusually quiet and a thick air of expectancy seemed to hover over the dusty streets, like a heavy, woollen blanket.

There weren't a lot of folks in the main street either, which was strange, as it was a Tuesday, a business day. They made a strange sight riding down the main street. Lars Beauchamp was still in his pyjamas, a blanket thrown around his shoulders, his hands tied to the pommel of his saddle and a rawhide rope tied around his waist with the loose end held firmly in the hand of a stern-faced Judge Whittiker.

They drew up outside the law office. Without dismounting the judge called out in a loud voice for Henry Dodds. All was quiet within the office for several moments, then the door slowly opened and Clem Abbots stepped out. He was wearing a badge.

'Well, Judge, we sure as hell were worried about you but it seems we didn't have to be. Looks like you went and caught this here wanted varmint all on your own.' He looked up at Carlos, a mean smile played at the corners of his mouth.

'Where's the sheriff and why are you out of jail?' The judge was indignant.

'Well, the sheriff's out looking for this half-breed desperado, and so he deputized me to look after things while he's gone. Freed me of all the trumped-up charges brought agin me by Carlos here also.'

Judge Whittiker looked across at Carlos. 'Well, Marshal, what are you waiting for? Arrest this killer.'

'You heard what the judge said, Abbots.

Drop your gun. I'm re-arresting you for murder.'

Cornered, Abbot was smart enough to realize that Dodds had set him up. His promise of immunity was worthless. Without warning his hand streaked for the Colt tied low on his hip, closed on the handle and began hauling iron. He wasn't fast enough. Carlos cleared leather before Abbots's gun was even halfway out of its holster. He shot him point blank in the shoulder. The heavy bullet fired at such close range knocked Abbots completely off his feet and he ended up lying hard against the jailhouse wall.

Carlos was off his horse instantly after firing that shot and he kicked the fallen man's gun aside. Without being too gentle he hauled him to his feet and pushed him into the jailhouse interior. He kept the momentum going, forcing the bleeding man back into an empty cell. When he was inside Carlos slammed the heavy iron door which locked itself with a loud metallic click.

'I need a doctor,' Abbots moaned, holding his wounded shoulder with blood running through his fingers.

'You'll get one, don't worry. You'll live to hang.'

Abbot's curses rang in his ears as he went outside for Beauchamp. A sizeable crowd of townsfolk had gathered as the judge, still astride his horse, explained what had happened. Carlos could see the mood of the crowd changing, becoming ugly towards Beauchamp, who decided he'd be safer inside keeping Abbots company.

As he escorted Beauchamp inside Pete Munny pushed through the crowd and stopped beside him.

'Can I help, Mr Williams?'

'Pete, lock Beauchamp in a cell and get the doc.'

He went back outside. Judge Whittiker was speaking, trying to quieten the crowd.

'I have sworn Carlos in as a United States marshal; he'll go after Henry Dodds and bring him back.'

Somebody yelled from the back to

get a rope and finish off the two inside.

The judge began to look nervous; this was growing worse by the moment. The young lawman stepped forward and addressed the angry faces. 'If any man tries to take the law into his own hands he'll be treated as a law-breaker. Now, who has any information on where Henry Dodds might be? Or when he was last seen?'

'Yesterday morning, I seen him and Nora Harding riding out of town heading west, figured they was just going riding. They been spooning for a while now.'

Nora Harding! So it appeared she really was in this also; Beauchamp had been right after all. Carlos suddenly felt sick to his stomach. 'Judge, I need to get some rest and then I'm going after them.'

'Where do you think they're headed, Carlos?'

'My guess would be California, but there's an awful lot of miles between here and there. I'll have time to catch them. Nora won't travel very well through the deserts of Arizona, she's used to town life. Now all you people get about your business and let the law do its job.' He was fast running out of patience.

There was a little bit of muttering but the crowd broke up and slowly dispersed.

Once back inside the jailhouse he saw that Pete had brought Doc Reynolds in through the back. The sawbones was already seeing to a groaning Clem Abbots.

Suddenly a thought occurred to Carlos and he went to the cell holding Lars Beauchamp.

'Where are the keys to your bank?'

'Back in my bedroom on the dresser.' Then his voice rose in panic. 'Why?'

Carlos didn't answer him but left the office, mounted the gelding and rode to Beauchamp's house.

He tied the horse at the picket gate, then circled the house looking for the place where Two Eagle Claws had gained entry the previous night. He soon found it. It was a small window at the rear, now in shade from the setting sun and hard to see.

Within moments he was inside the neat little clapboard house and had found his way to the dresser. No matter where he looked, however, he couldn't find the keys. He searched almost every-where he thought the banker might be likely to have put them but came up empty-handed every time. Then a light went on in his head.

He left the house, mounted the gelding once more and headed for the bank.

The front of the bank was securely locked, probably just as Lars had left it when he'd locked up after closing the other night, so he made his way to the rear.

The back door was shut but not locked, which in itself seemed suspicious; it allowed him to gain easy access from the rear into the office. Like Beauchamp's house, the office was neat, comfortable, but not extravagant.

Carlos made his way over to the west wall into which the big vault was set. It stood open, open and empty of any cash, notes or coin. He saw what he had suspected to see so left the room and headed back to the jail, thanking his lucky stars that he had drawn all his cash out when he had.

'There was gold bullion in that safe, twenty bars of it,' a crestfallen Lars explained when he learned that Henry and Nora had high-tailed it with the contents of his safe, and worse, left him to face the music.

Through a pain-racked explanation from Abbots, they also learned that Dodds had assured Abbots he would be granted immunity and a pardon for his part in the crimes if he took over the role of deputy.

Dodds had played everyone for a fool but Carlos was determined to go after him and Nora.

Suddenly the room swam slightly and the new Marshal knew he had to get some sleep. 'Judge, I'm going over to the hotel to grab something to eat, get cleaned up a bit then sleep till the morning, and then I'll go after him.'

As he reached the door a sudden thought struck him; he turned back. 'Judge, if young Pete Munny here is interested it might pay to offer him the deputy's job while I'm away. Someone needs to be left to look after the town. Owl hoots hear there's no law in Big Springs and they'll start to mosey in looking for easy pickings.' Carlos, with a grin, looked with interest at the young man.

19

The next morning, after a good night's sleep and with a hefty breakfast on board he rode from the livery stable leading yet another packhorse. It had been well looked after and fed on oats so it was at first a skittish handful. Carlos expertly used the big sorrel to crowd the feisty beast until he settled down.

Outside the jailhouse he met Pete Munny; if his grin had been any wider it would have split his face in half.

'Mornin', Marshal Williams.'

'Morning, Deputy. Seen the judge yet?'

'Yes, he'll be over shortly, I believe he's signing the arrest warrants.'

Even as they spoke the figure of Judge Whittiker hurried importantly towards them. He was out of breath and mopping at his face with a white handkerchief. He nodded to Pete before addressing the marshal.

'Carlos.' He dug in his pocket and brought out a marshal's badge. 'Wear this with pride. It's the symbol of law and order that's coming to these parts. There will always be men like Henry Dodds who start out with the right intentions but greed or some other obstruction gets in their way and they stumble. Don't stumble, Carlos; help change the West for the better.'

He thrust the arrest warrants into the other's hand.

'I'll sure do my best, Judge.' He turned to Pete. 'Practise with that gun you got there because you may need it.'

'You take care of yourself, Marshal, Sheriff Dodds is a desperate man and I don't think he'll take to kindly to being captured.'

Carlos headed west towards the border between Texas and New Mexico, which he would have to cross completely before reaching Arizona. He would have to cross that state too, before eventually reaching California. If he thought the journey after Bishop and Abbots had been a long one, then that was nothing compared to this.

He had to travel clear across two whole states and they were made up of the most fearsome and unforgiving land in the whole of the United States.

Deserts, prairies and more deserts. Scorching sun, rattlesnakes and scorpions, dried up waterholes and lonely mountains and canyons. But it had to be done. On the way out of town he looked to the ridge and saw the lonely figure on horseback watching him. He raised his hand in silent salute and saw Two Eagle Claw turn his horse and disappear.

As he rode he thought of Nora Harding and wondered how strong her love must be for Henry Dodds that she would travel through the bowels of hell with him. Or was she just in so deep that she must of necessity hitch her wagon to his star?

Carlos figured the fugitives' first stop would be El Paso; that was where he hoped to pick up their trail.

It would be an unusual sight for a man and woman to be travelling together on horseback through the inhospitable lands of the south-west. Someone was bound to remember them.

In the dusty, sleepy little town of El Paso, in a dirty little cantina, and for the price of three dollars, he learned that two people, a man and a woman, fitting the description of Henry and Nora, had passed through on their way west three days before. They had stopped long enough to fill their water bottles, eat, and then they were gone.

From El Paso he headed north-west towards Las Cruces, about forty miles as the crow flies, where he would pick up the main trail west to California.

There were a mighty lot of towns on the way, both big and small. Unfortunately, he might have to look in all of them, just in case his quarry had decided to stop.

Henry had plenty of cash on him and he could afford to think of starting afresh in such places as Tucson or Phoenix, though Carlos doubted it.

He guessed they would head for San Diego and if Henry Dodds didn't feel safe there he could board a ship for parts unknown and never be heard of again, never having to answer for his crimes.

Carlos was determined to step up his pursuit and catch them before that could happen, even if it meant riding day and night until he dropped.

Las Cruces gave him nothing new, except that a couple, a man and woman, had stopped here and the man had bought fresh horses. Carlos too was forced to do the same, keeping the gelding but trading the packhorse for a large, raw-boned mule.

He rode out of Las Cruces on the fleet-footed gelding, leading the mule. It was feisty and mean but better able to handle the weight of the supplies that Carlos topped up from the only store the town offered, and better able to stand the raw, hostile land they would now be passing through.

The days were hot as fire but the nights came with a drop in temperature that was bitterly cold.

He picked his night camps in the canyons that abounded in southern Arizona, so that he could build a fire without the worry of its being seen by hostile eyes.

He reached the town of Lordsburg in the late afternoon on what he thought was a Thursday, which meant he had been on their trail for five days. He still had another twenty or so miles to go to reach Arizona. Finding the livery stable he saw to the horse's and mule's needs before he went looking for the sheriff's office.

He needed a bath and a decent meal but decided to seek out the town's lawman more as a token of respect than in any hope of getting some more helpful information, before he ate and freshened himself up.

The sheriff's name was Joel Briggin. He seemed more than happy to hear the story Carlos told him, though he had nothing to add to what the lawman from Big Springs already knew, or didn't know, about the final destination of Henry and Nora.

'I knew Henry a few years back. He was a good man, too bad he's turned maverick. Anyway, Marshal, I have to do my rounds, so if you'll excuse me, you know how it is?' He shrugged beefy shoulders in apology and stepped aside, ushering Carlos to the heavy door.

'Well, thanks for your help, Sheriff. Which is the best hotel in town? I reckon I'll stay the night in a hotel for once; riding the trail can get to a fella after a while.'

'The Shamrock, run by Mrs Sally Jamieson, a widder woman. It's about the best in town, Marshal; at least you'll get a clean bed and decent food.'

Five minutes later he signed the register under the watchful eye of a very pretty Sally Jamieson, who looked to be in her early thirties, not the old widow Carlos had imagined.

'Where can I get a bath, ma'am?' he asked, aware of her scrutiny.

'I'll have the porter draw one for you in your room.' She looked down at the register. 'Mr Williams.'

'Is the kitchen still open, ma'am? I could sure use some food other than what I've cooked myself these last few days.'

'You clean yourself up, Mr Williams, and by the time you come downstairs I'll have steak and eggs and coffee all ready for you.'

He smiled his gratitude at her. Suddenly, looking at her, he felt a sadness sweep over him that she could not help but see. It had been a long time now since he'd been in a pretty woman's company, especially one who was obviously willing to take this new acquaintance a little further.

He thought of Nadie, but then, even surprising himself, the face of Leosanni swam before his eyes. After taking the key she handed him he turned away and headed up the stairs to his room.

He felt relaxed for the first time in a

long while as he lay soaking in the hot bath, so relaxed that he didn't hear the quiet knock nor hear the door open. When she spoke his hand streaked for the gun hanging on a stand just above the bath. He didn't think — or at least hoped — it wasn't the fact of his nudity as he leapt to his feet, revolver in hand, cascading water everywhere, that made her drop the plate of food. Probably it was the fact that she was staring down the barrel of a gun. She must have thought that this was the nearest she had come to dying in her life.

With a muffled cry she turned and fled from the room.

He quickly towelled himself dry, dressed, then picked up the plate and headed downstairs. She was behind the counter. When she looked up at him he could see the embarrassment in her face.

'Well, ma'am, that isn't the first time a pretty lady has seen me buck naked. Hell, my mother did for many years. Mind you, she never dropped plates of food at the shock of it.'

'I'm sorry, you must think me terrible?'

'No, of course not, no harm done.'

'You're very kind, Mr Williams. If you go into the dining room I'll get you some more hot food. There's plenty of steak and eggs and the coffee's still on the stove.'

'Well thank you, ma'am, that sounds mighty nice.' With a mock bow and flourish, he went into the dining room and found he was the only one there; it was eight o'clock so all the other diners must have already eaten. A few minutes later she came to his table and handed him a glass of whiskey. 'It's on the house, Mr Williams; help you sleep. By the way, I've moved your things into another room and the porter will clean up the spilled food.'

She was gone before he could thank her.

After the excellent, well-cooked meal she brought him more coffee. Just looking at her, her softness and femininity brought feelings to him that he would just as soon have kept buried. He longed for the touch of a woman, for he missed Nadie so much, but the face of Leosanni was before him now, more and more often.

With some reluctance he asked for the keys to the new room and mumbled an explanation about being up early on the trail.

'Sheriff Briggin was asking after you earlier.'

'He was? What did he want?'

'Oh nothing really, just to make sure you were OK, said you'd been through a lot recently, asked what room I'd put you in and whether you were comfortable.'

'Well, that was mighty nice of him. Does he know I've changed rooms?'

'No, he came in before . . . ' She looked away.

'Ma'am, I'd surely appreciate it if it stayed that way. Do you mind?'

'No, of course not. You get a good night's rest, Mr Williams. I'll have breakfast ready for you at six. Goodnight.'

'Goodnight ma'am.' For the second

time he went up the stairs. He found the room, two doors down and on the other side of the hall. Letting himself in, he removed his hat, boots and gunbelt but took the gun out of the holster and put it under the pillow. Then, without removing his clothes, he lay down on the bed. Within minutes he was asleep.

He didn't remember falling asleep but he was suddenly awakened by he shattering roar of a six-shooter. He was off the bed pronto, and with gun in hand, he headed for the door and quietly opened it.

Another door further down the hall opened and Sally Jamieson appeared, holding a lantern and looking scared. Carlos beckoned to her to bring the light and she was quickly beside him, trembling like a leaf in a strong wind. He held his finger to his lips indicating silence and softly made his way down the hall. The strong, acrid smell of gun smoke still lingering in the air told him that the shooting had come from the room he had originally been given. The room he should have been staying in.

Softly he turned the door handle and gingerly peered into the room; the shooter was gone. The window leading to a balcony that ran around the front of the hotel was open and the pillow where his head would have been was covered in feathers from the bullets that had entered it.

'My God, who could have done this?'

There was noise from the street as sleepy-eyed townsfolk gathered in a group outside the hotel.

'I think I know the answer to that. How long has Briggin been sheriff?'

She looked puzzled. 'About a year. You don't think . . . ?'

'Well, who else in town knew which room I should have been staying in?'

She thought about his statement 'Yes, you're right. What do you intend to do now?'

He frowned and thought about that for a moment. He had to catch the sheriff and arrest him or kill him. He couldn't have him dogging his trail, looking for another opportunity to gun him down as he searched for Dodds.

It was clear that Dodds had put the man up to it, probably paid him a good chunk of cash to murder the lawman from Big Springs, which also proved that Dodds knew Carlos would come after him. There would probably be a gunnie hired by Dodds in all the towns from here to California. Dodds had virtually put a price on the head of Carlos; maybe it was only a matter of time before someone collected.

'Any chance of a coffee, ma'am?' He broke the tense silence and she smiled at him.

She led him downstairs to the kitchen. The little Alpine, chalet-carved cuckoo clock on the wall told him it was 5.30 in the morning.'

'Well, I promised to have breakfast for you at six, Mr Williams, so I might as well start.'

He smiled at her as she prepared the

coffee. 'That was one hell of a wake-up call, ma'am. I guess I owe you my life. Thanks!'

He headed back upstairs for his boots, gunbelt and saddle-bags. When he returned the coffee was ready and the smell of bacon and eggs frying sure made him glad to be alive. No thanks to Briggin.

There was a sudden knocking on the front door and Sally went to open it. She came back a little while later with a tall, thin man who introduced himself as Tobias Collins the town mayor, and with him was Sheriff Joel Briggin.

When the reason for the gunplay was explained Briggin suggested that he should take a look in the room for any clues the would-be assassin might have left behind, and disappeared upstairs.

Sally offered the mayor a coffee as they sat at the kitchen table. Carlos explained the reasons why he was here and whom he was searching for, saying that Briggin had claimed he hadn't seen them. This brought a gasp of disbelief from Sally. 'Why, the three of them were in here day before yesterday. They had a meal together.'

'Do you know when they left?'

'Early yesterday morning, first light.'

This merely confirmed Carlos's belief that Dodds had paid another lawman to kill him and he told them of his suspicions.

Tobias Collins looked steadily at Carlos for a few moments. 'What do you intend to do with Sheriff Briggin, Marshal?'

'Well, if he hasn't already jumped out of the window and high-tailed it for parts unknown, I'll arrest him and charge him with attempted murder and lock him up here until I get back.'

They heard footsteps on the stairs and moments later Briggin entered the kitchen.

'Well, whoever it was they're long gone. Guess we'll never know.'

Carlos stood up away from the table, his hand dangling at his side ready for whatever might Briggin might decide to do. 'How much did he pay you to kill me, Sheriff?'

A startled look crossed Briggin's face, then, seeing he'd been caught out, his hand dropped to his gun. He was fast, he had it out and was beginning to line it up on Carlos when Carlos's own gun spoke first. The heavy .44 slug took Briggin just under the heart and his legs folded under him.

He was dead when he hit the floor.

Carlos supposed that the reason Briggin had not cleared out was the fact that he didn't think he was a suspect and hadn't realized that he was the only person, apart from Sally Jamieson, who knew the marshal was even in town.

Whatever the reason, it had cost him his life. Carlos holstered his gun and looked at the others. Their faces were shocked, and they wouldn't meet his gaze.

20

He left the town of Lordsburg after replenishing his supplies. He knew they were glad to see him go. A man with death clinging to him like a bad smell isn't really welcome in too many places.

As he drew ever closer to the border with Arizona, huge saguaro cactus and agaves began to dot the countryside and that old devil sun was still doing his best to fry his brain. Already his shirt was rimed with sweat-stains and he would have to stop every now and then to rinse out the animals' nostrils and water them from one of the extra canteens which he poured into his Stetson, a new one without any bullet holes.

But at least now he knew he could be no more than perhaps a day behind them.

His mood, however, was sombre as

his thoughts dwelt on the fact that another man had died, caught up in a game that was not of his making. Still, Briggin had decided to play and the game was a tough one.

The next town of any size was Benson, about a hundred miles or so away. He was debating with himself whether or not to bypass it and head straight to Tucson, just in case someone else was waiting there to plug him, and perhaps this time might be lucky, when the dazzling sunlight danced on something up ahead.

For a moment he thought he was seeing things but no; a pair of small-sized boots lay in the sand just as if they'd been tossed there by a child in a tantrum. Further on was a pair of jeans and close after that a woman's blouse, then a hat. If it had come to this then Henry and Nora were in big trouble.

Then he saw the buzzards circling in the distance. Buzzards out here in the badlands of Arizona meant only one thing; something was already dead, or it was dying. He didn't have long to find out what. Twenty minutes later he came across the body of a horse.

It had been dead for maybe a day or less, so there was still plenty for the birds to eat and pick at. They didn't like the fact that he had disturbed them at their grisly meal and hissed and flapped at him as he rode closer to take a look.

As he drew nearer they took to the air with angry squawks. It was then that he saw the small, naked body of Nora Harding, lying on the other side of the horse.

The buzzards had got to her also, her eyes were gone and so too her lips and ears but they hadn't obliterated the small, neat bullet hole in the middle of her forehead.

So he had killed her too. Carlos felt the anger born of hopelessness well up within him. Suddenly he hated Henry Dodds, hated him with a hatred that left him frightened and shaking.

Something had happened. Had she

lost her mind in the searing heat? Had she been innocent in all this and had somehow found out what Henry had become and had tried to stop him?

He dismounted and went over to where she lay. The answer hit him almost immediately. He bent down, picked up her canteen and shook it, it was bone dry. There were no other containers lying around, so Henry had taken them all and had continued on.

Henry should have known better, but then he had been a *town* sheriff for many years and hadn't had to take a hard trail in a mighty long time. Also, a horse can only take so much weight in country like this and it sure looked like Henry fully intended to take the gold as well as the water. It seemed the gold had robbed him of every spark of common sense he had ever had.

He picked up the fleeing lawman's trail about four hours after burying Nora.

Dodds was now on foot and leading his horse. His footsteps and those of his mount meandered like a sidewinder with a sore belly and Carlos, following the tracks, realized that something was seriously wrong.

His guess would be that in the heat Henry's hip was playing him up, so he slowed up his travel, knowing that the man he sought wasn't all that far ahead.

He found him an hour later, sitting beside his fallen horse, his head in his hands.

'Henry, I've come to take you back.'

Henry looked up through eyes squinting against the glare of the sun. He appeared spent and haggard.

'Carlos, I knew if anyone could find me it would be you. Didn't think it would be this soon though.'

'Why did you do it, Henry? Why did you do any of it?'

'I was sheriff of Big Springs for a mighty long time, Carlos, and they owed me something.'

'What did I ever owe you, Henry? What did Nadie or Nairn ever owe you?'

'That was a mistake; they were never meant to get hurt; thought they were elsewhere.'

'But you didn't mistake Dunsford or Jeb Claiborne; you just murdered them because you wanted what they had.'

'Hell, Carlos, they fought back. Jeb, well, he recognized me so he had to go. My hip was playing me up something fearful. What was I going to do when it stopped me from working, stopped me from being sheriff? Hell's fire, there wasn't even a pension to fall back on and there was no savings.'

'What about Nora? She loved you enough to go with you. You could have married her, and she had her shop?'

Henry looked surprised. 'What, live off a woman? Ain't ever have and never will.'

'Why did you kill her? Why did she have to die?'

Carlos felt the anger was beginning to melt away as he looked at this pathetic figure sitting dumbly in the Arizonan desert beside a dead horse with thousands of dollars worth of cash and gold in the heavy saddle-bags, all of it about as much use to him as a cup of sand to a thirsty man.

Suddenly Henry Dodds began to sob. 'We was running low on water and I was trying to conserve what little we had left, doling it out little by little, but it wasn't enough and eventually the heat got her, sent her crazy. First she started taking her clothes off, one by one, then she began babbling and screaming, begging for water, then she just fell down and refused to move. I had to do it, I couldn't just leave her there.'

They were still more than three days' ride from Benson and that was where they still needed to go. Carlos would have to pick up another horse for Dodds and another mule to carry the gold back. The gold and money had to go back to Big Springs or a lot of folk there would be financially ruined.

'Drop your gunbelt, Henry, nice and slow; unbuckle it with your left hand.' There was iron in his voice. However, all the fight seemed to have gone out of Henry Dodds and suddenly, as Carlos looked down at him, he saw him for the first time as he really was, a broken, frightened old man.

'What you aiming to do, Carlos?'

'We'll leave everything here and go into Benson, get another horse for you, another mule to carry the gold then we're going back to Big Springs. You have to face up to what you've done. Henry.'

'They'll hang me, Carlos.'

'That would be my guess too, but you've got it coming, Henry.'

Carlos dismounted, keeping a wary eye on the other man, and picked up his gun belt; he also took the Spencer rifle from the saddle boot. Pathetic, beaten or not, armed, Henry was still a dangerous man.

He unloaded the mule and put the packs a few feet away from the horse. He covered them with his slicker, then he went to Henry's dead mount and undid the saddle-bags. There were four of them and they were heavy with the gold inside. Carlos placed them with the other things, using their weight to keep the slicker pegged to the ground.

'What if somebody comes by? They'll get all that gold.'

'I guess they will, but let's hope no one does, I'd hate to lose a good raincoat.'

Henry didn't try anything the rest of the way to Benson, even though they didn't reach it until late afternoon of the fourth day. Carlos had kept Dodds legs shackled throughout the nights, so he wouldn't be tempted to try anything.

Carlos supposed the older man might wait until he'd regained some of his strength back and try to escape on the way back home. It didn't matter; he wasn't going to be out of sight, and Carlos really wanted to take him back alive.

Riding into Benson they created a bit of a stir. A tall, lean man, with long dark hair wearing a United States marshal's badge pinned to his calico shirt, every bit an Indian, riding a big, tired horse and leading a white man shackled and tied to a mule were bound to arouse curiosity. They made their way to the sheriff's office.

It seemed that this was all Carlos's life had become: chasing wanted men and spending most of his time visiting or leaving a jailhouse.

Word must have got to the sheriff long before they reached him, for a short, squat man stepped out of the shadows of an alleyway with a ten-gauge scatter-gun held tightly across his chest, the wicked twin barrels pointed right at the two mounted men.

'Hold it right there, gents, this shotgun has a hair trigger.'

'Afternoon, Sheriff. I'm Carlos Williams, marshal from Big Springs Texas. This here's Henry Dodds. I'm taking him back to answer murder charges and would be mighty obliged if I could have the use of one of your cells while I get a few things and rest up a spell.'

'You got any papers sayin' to that

effect, marshal?'

Carlos carefully reached his hand into his shirt pocket and heard the familiar click as Benson's sheriff cocked back the hammers on the shotgun. 'Nice and easy, son. I'd sure hate to drop another lawman; look bad on my record.'

He was handed the warrants sworn out by Judge Whittiker.

He studied them for several moments, then looked up at Henry, then at Carlos.

'Where's this Nora Harding woman?'

'Back on the trail a ways. Henry here, put a bullet through her head.'

'I guess you better come in and tell me all about it, marshal.' He swung the gun away and they proceeded to the jailhouse. On the way in he introduced himself as Sheriff Pat Conroy.

Inside it was cool and dark. After Henry had been placed in a cell and the door securely locked, he wearily sat on the bunk and asked for a drink of water.

The sheriff gave him a cupful. After drinking it down the exhausted man lay on the cot and went to sleep.

Carlos drank the last of the strong black coffee and finished explaining the events that had led to him and Henry Dodds being here in the town of Benson.

'Well, that's quite a story, Carlos,' the lawman opined. 'There's always a rotten stink when a lawman turns bad, but I guess greed can work at a man like a canker until it just drives him plumb loco.'

'I think you've just about got it right, Pat. Henry used to be one hell of a good lawman, but right now all I want to do is have something to eat, grab some rest and take him back.'

Carlos hadn't mentioned the fact that they had left all that gold behind. Why would he? Maybe that would be enough for this lawman, too, to turn outlaw. It was getting that he didn't want to trust anyone any more.

The next morning, after feeding the prisoner, Carlos sat eating some beef and beans with the sheriff. When he'd finished he set off to the livery stable to get a mount for Henry and another mule to help carry the gold back.

He selected a little bay mare for Henry. She was strong of wind but not strong enough to outrun the gelding should Henry try to escape on the way back.

He couldn't get another mule, so he opted for a large mare that looked like she'd go the distance and then some.

Then he stopped in at the general mercantile store for more supplies: bacon, coffee, hardtack. He also bought two extra canteens. After paying for everything he took his purchases outside and loaded up the saddle-bags on all three horses.

There were still supplies back where they had left everything, but desert creatures have a way of getting into things left unattended. They couldn't spoil the gold but they could sure as hell chew through the vittles.

He led the horses back to the jailhouse, hitched them to the post outside, then went up the two wooden stairs to the jailhouse door. It was shut so he pushed it open and stepped inside, closing it behind him.

He sensed a movement to his left from behind the closing door, then something hit him across the back of the head. Brilliantly coloured stars bounced in every direction from inside his skull as his legs sagged and he lost consciousness.

When he came to sometime later he found himself in the cell previously occupied by Henry Dodds.

He tried sitting up and felt instantly nauseous. The pain in his head convinced him something in there must be broken. His mouth was dry; he needed a drink. With sheer, stubborn, effort of will he forced himself to sit up, groaning silently with the pain and holding his head in case it fell apart.

His movements brought a man he hadn't seen before into the cells. He was wearing a deputy's badge. 'Don't try nothin smart, mister, Sheriff Conroy sez you're a dangerous crimnal and I'm to blast you if you try anythin'.'

'Water, I need some water.' The deputy was gone for a few moments then came back with a tin cup full of water.

'Move to the back of the cell, Mr Dodds, where I can keep an eye on you.'

Dodds! Hell! suddenly Carlos saw what had happened while he'd been away getting the supplies. He had to hand it to Henry, the man was sure inventive.

He gingerly moved to the back of the cell, as the deputy put the cup down close to the bars on the other side and quickly stepped back. 'The sheriff sez you're a dangerous killer.'

The water made Carlos feel better and the throbbing in his head was easing off a bit.

'What's your name, Deputy?'

'Hank.'

'Where's Sheriff Conroy, Hank, and the man he had with him?'

'You mean Marshal Williams? They've gone out to bring back the body of that woman you killed back on the trail a ways as evidence before they hang you.'

Carlos could only shake his head at how quickly Henry had been believed by the other man, Pat Conroy. It was ironical really and as Western as desert and rattlesnakes and cactus. Carlos was part Indian, worse, he was part Apache and that made him, in the eyes of some, immediately guilty.

Henry was a white man; it had been easy for him to convince Conroy that Carlos had got the drop on him out on the trail and had swapped names in the hope of seeing Henry held captive while he, Carlos, got away.

Pat Conroy was a dead man. As soon as they were far enough away Dodds would kill him and escape. Suddenly Carlos gripped the bars in anger and tried to shake the immovable metal door in his fury and frustration.

Hank's eyes widened in fear. 'Now you just quit that there, Mr Dodds. That's solid steel. Ain't no ways you're gonna bust that down.'

'Hank, how long ago did they leave?'

'About two hours. Said they'd be back by nightfall.'

'Hank, they're not coming back. If Conroy's not already dead then he soon will be.'

'How's that? What you talking about? He went off with Sheriff Williams, another lawman. What you trying to pull?' A veil of suspicion crossed his face, and Carlos realized that Hank was a little slow, but he was the only chance Carlos had of getting out of here.

'Hank, did they show you the arrest warrants?'

'Well, no I guess they didn't. Just told me to watch you until they got back.'

'Is there a telegraph office here?'

'What you trying to pull, Mr Dodds?'

'Hank, go over to the telegraph office and send a cable to Judge Whittiker back in Big Springs. Tell him what's happened and describe the man now sitting in this cell to him. There may still be time to save the life of your sheriff.'

'Well, I don't know.' He hesitated,

clearly undecided what to do. 'Sheriff Conroy said not to take my eye off'n you as you're so dangerous and all.'

'Do you like the sheriff, Hank?'

'Sure do. He's the fella what gave me this job being deputy.'

'Well, Hank, if you want to see him alive again will you do as I ask? It won't take you long and hell, I'm not really going anywhere now, am I?'

He could almost see the conflict going on inside the deputy's mind. Hank had been told to stay put by the man he liked and looked up to; on the other hand there was a chance this man they had locked up could be telling the truth and that would put Conroy in terrible danger.

Suddenly the deputy made up his mind. 'I'll do it, but if you're playing games you'll be mighty sorry.'

Carlos breathed a sigh of relief. 'Hurry, man. There's no time to lose.'

Hank was gone for about twenty minutes, then returned, letting himself in through the front door of the jail-house with a huge key. He came to the cell door as Carlos sat up from the cot. 'I sent it off like you asked; the clerk said he'd send the reply over the minute he received it, so I guess we'll just have to wait. You hungry?'

There was a mouth-watering smell of bacon and brewing coffee wafting around the jailhouse ten minutes later.

While they ate Carlos asked Hank how the conversation had gone between Conroy and Dodds.

'Well, they both got to talkin' about bygone days and bad men they had known and it seems they knew quite a few between them.'

As Hank talked Carlos could see how easy it would have been for Dodds to convince Conroy that he, Dodds, was the peace officer taking back the renegade Apache 'breed, and had been captured instead when his guard had been down.

They had just finished eating when there was a knock on the door and a little man with a stooped back entered. He had an air of importance about him that snapped Hank to attention. He didn't bother handing the cable to Hank, he just looked quietly at him as he spoke.

'Hank, if you want to see Sheriff Conroy alive again you better let Marshal Williams here out of jail, and pray to God we're not too late.'

21

Carlos soon picked up their trail. Two horses carrying riders, plus a third horse being led. Carlos was sure that the third horse would be for the gold, not to bring back Nora's body.

This time Carlos didn't ride alone. Deputy Hank Felden rode with him; he was determined now to either help Williams arrest Henry Dodds, or, as he said with a catch in his voice, bring back the body of Sheriff Pat Conroy for a decent Christian burial.

For Carlos it was simply a matter of heading back to where they had left the cache of gold, Nora and the dead horse, so he didn't have to spend valuable time looking for sign. He knew exactly where Henry Dodds was headed.

They kept at a steady ground-eating lope, trying to cut the distance down between themselves and the other two, until something loomed up on the trail ahead. Both men sawed hard at the reins of the running horses to stop them trampling over the prostrate form of Pat Conroy.

Carlos, lighter and more athletic, was out of the saddle before the gelding stopped moving. He ran to the downed man. A quick look told him the sheriff was just barely alive. His breathing was shallow and the red stain on his back told Carlos where he had been shot. Conroy's eyes flickered open and he looked at Carlos from a grey, ashen face. When he spoke his voice was hoarse. 'I reckon I threw my rope over the wrong bronco, son.'

'Easy!' Carlos told him. 'Don't try to talk.'

Hank arrived with a water bottle and together they managed to get some fluid into the badly wounded man, though the effort caused him to choke. However, it seemed to revive him a little and he stirred himself.

'Do you think you can stand,

Sheriff?' Hank asked.

'I'll sure try; don't fancy being a meal for the buzzards.'

Carlos turned to Hank. 'Help me get him mounted, then take him back. If he's lucky he'll make it.'

'But what happened?' Hank was stupefied, dumbfounded to find the sheriff like this.

'Hank, I haven't got time to explain it and I don't need Conroy to tell me because I know what happened. Now get him back to a doctor before he bleeds to death.'

Carlos climbed on board the gelding and handed the reins of the packhorse to Hank. It would carry the sheriff now and not the gold, the bay he would take with him.

'Look after that horse, Hank, I might come back for him some day.' Before Hank could reply, Carlos was already on his way.

Soon he came upon the spot where they had left the dead horse, gold, and provisions, under the yellow slicker.

The gold was gone and the provisions, those that Dodds couldn't use or take with him, he'd ripped apart and strewn over the sandy ground, leaving nothing of worth uncontaminated by sand.

It didn't bother Carlos all that much, he had enough in his saddle-bags, but it did make him angry, and any vestige of pity he might have felt before for Henry evaporated like the sweat on his handsome face.

His guess was that now Dodds would head south-east for Tombstone, then to Bisbee, heading for the Rio Grande and the Mexican border.

In Mexico with that much gold he could live like a king, hire himself an army for protection and no one would be able to touch him.

Carlos could see that the horse he led, the one with the gold bars in its saddle-bags was sinking quite deeply into the soft desert sand. If Dodds maintained the pace he was setting at the moment for any length of time he would run that horse into the ground. In his desire to get away he wasn't taking into account the country he was travelling through. It had almost got him once already but he obviously hadn't learned any lessons. Carlos felt he could ease up a little because sooner or later, before Henry could get within a lightning strike of Tombstone, Carlos was going to catch up to him.

He topped a slight rise and was able to see through the shimmering heat haze a fair distance ahead. Nothing moved!

The tracks left by the quickly tiring, heavily laden horse, were digging deeper and deeper into the ground as the animal was forced to use up ever more energy under that weight of gold he was carrying without let-up. Carlos knew it was only a matter of time before the horse collapsed. As darkness was only an hour or so away, he decided to find a sheltered spot to put up for the night and resume the trail again tomorrow.

He stripped down the horses, washed the sand and grit from their nostrils which made them snort appreciatively, then he gave them water. After rope-hobbling the animals he turned them loose to graze through the yucca and ocotillo.

With the Rincon mountain range as a backdrop he settled into a large depression in the otherwise flat ground and began preparing a meal of fried bacon and eggs. The coffee pot was soon bubbling away.

As he ate he watched the setting sun paint the western sky in colours so brilliant it almost hurt his eyes. Away in the distance a coyote called, his lonesome voice raised to the heavens. The coyote put sound to the sadness that was still deep in the soul of Carlos Williams. It was as if the creature understood the man's misery and sang his mournful song in sympathy for the lone lawman camped out under the starry night.

The next morning, once he had seen to the horses and eaten a cold breakfast of hardtack washed down with cold, black coffee, he saddled up and began once again to track Henry Dodds.

It didn't take long to pick up Dodds trail, and after a few hours he found the spot where the fugitive had laid up for the night. Gold can do funny things to a man and Carlos could easily tell, by the deep hoof impressions that Dodds hadn't even bothered to take the heavy bags of gold from the back of the horse overnight, which meant the horse had not rested as he should.

Carlos began to sense that he might catch up to Dodds within the next hour or two, perhaps no more than three. He took his Winchester from its boot and checked the workings, levering a round into the chamber.

The packhorse Henry had used to carry the gold was the first thing Carlos saw as he topped a slight rise in the otherwise table-flat country. The animal had played out at last, dropping dead from sheer exhaustion.

He slipped lithely from his own horse

and went, bent double, to the side of the fallen beast. It hadn't died all that long ago for the vultures hadn't yet discovered it, so Henry wasn't all that far away. A quick search through the saddle-bags told him the gold, all of it, was gone. That meant that Dodds had overloaded the other horse and that horse would fare no better than this one lying dead before him.

He raised his head to scan the distant horizon for any speck of movement when a bullet, with the noise of an angry wasp whacked through the air inches from his head. He flattened himself down, using the dead horse as cover. He hadn't even seen where the bullet came from. He was reluctant to raise his head again to try and see because the next bullet might be better aimed. He took off his hat and slowly raised it from behind the dead creature's bulk.

Boom!

He judged from the loudness of the shot that the shooter wasn't very far away. The only cover he had seen before being shot at was a little stand of agaves and yucca plants, fifty feet off to his right and slightly ahead.

He began to dig the sandy ground away from under the dead mount's neck. He worked steadily in the scorching heat until he had dug a hole deep enough to easily take his head and shoulders while allowing him to be under the horse's thick neck, using that for protection. He was able now to scan those bushes safely for any hint of movement.

It wasn't long in coming. Dodds was lying under the same scorching sun that was making the ground shimmer, only he wasn't able to stand its heat without moving, like Carlos. He wriggled a little to the left, looking for more shade from the sparse plants from which he had chosen to launch his ambush.

Carlos sent a bullet towards the movement, but not really aiming. He heard a startled grunt; it must have been close.

'Carlos, let's do a deal?'

'No deal, Henry. I'm taking you back

this time dead or alive. The choice is up to you.'

'That ain't much of a choice, son.'

'It's the only one you're getting, Henry.'

Another shot and the chestnut gelding Carlos had ridden all those miles, screamed and went down.

'By God, Henry.' His words of frustrated anger were torn away as another blast rent the still desert air and a bullet winged away to Carlos's left.

Carlos answered with three quick rounds pumped at where he thought the shot had came from, but the only result he received was silence.

After firing, Carlos lay still under the broiling sun, trying to conserve the moisture being sucked steadily from his body.

'For Gawd's sake, Carlos, we can work this out, man. We've known each other for a long time. Hell, we used to be good friends.'

Something was wrong. Henry's voice reached Carlos from a different direction, and he saw that Henry was trying to work his way around him and get behind, maybe going for the bay.

'Our friendship died the night you killed my wife and her brother.'

There was silence and Carlos began to look quickly around, having to raise his head slightly as he did so.

Whang! A bullet thudded into the dead horse's neck mere inches from Carlos head. Carlos replied with two shots of his own.

Suddenly a scream of rage rent the air and Henry burst from cover twenty yards to the left from where Carlos lay. As he came he pumped shot after shot at the prone man. The fact that he was running, screaming as he came, made his shots pepper the ground harmlessly away from where Carlos lay.

Carlos had all the time in the world to take steady aim and fire at Dodds as the man charged recklessly towards him. The heavy bullet took Henry Dodds cleanly in the middle of his chest and stopped him dead in his tracks. His legs buckled and he was flung backwards.

Several tense seconds went by before Carlos moved. Henry lay where he had fallen, dead.

Just like that, it was all over. Carlos knelt down and looked sadly at the dead man. Particles of sand were already beginning to cover his face.

He went looking for Henry's horse. He found the animal standing with hanging head in a clump of tall saguaro cactus where Henry had left him tied. The first thing Carlos did was relieve the horse of its heavy load of gold, letting the saddlebags lie where they fell. Then he gave the thirsty animal some water.

After he'd buried Henry and allowed the horse to rest awhile he meant to start back to Big Springs. He could take back the cash Henry had stolen to the people it belonged to. At least the paper notes weighed next to nothing, but he would bury the gold at a spot he would remember, making a map and someone could come back and get it.

At last all was done. Henry was buried; and the gold too, at a spot Carlos drew on a scrap of paper. He had dug a hole for the gold beside the dead gelding, knowing that the bones, or hopefully most of them would remain fairly close to where the horse itself now lay. Once the bones were found then the map he had drawn would be easy enough to read and whoever was sent back to get it shouldn't have too much difficulty.

After gathering up all the water he could find and carry he began slowly walking, leading the exhausted horse in a direction that would eventually take them both to Big Springs. From there he intended to start up his ranch again.

He was sure it was what Nadie would have wanted. He also knew that Nadie would not want him to be lonely, pining away, becoming old and bitter.

There was someone he knew his Nadie would approve of and when he got back to his Apache family he fully intended courting her, if she'd still have him.

We do hope that you have enjoyed reading this large print book.

Did you know that all of our titles are available for purchase?

We publish a wide range of high quality large print books including:
Romances, Mysteries, Classics
General Fiction
Non Fiction and Westerns

Special interest titles available in large print are:
The Little Oxford Dictionary
Music Book, Song Book
Hymn Book, Service Book

Also available from us courtesy of Oxford University Press:
Young Readers' Dictionary
(large print edition)
Young Readers' Thesaurus
(large print edition)

For further information or a free brochure, please contact us at:
Ulverscroft Large Print Books Ltd.,
The Green, Bradgate Road, Anstey,
Leicester, LE7 7FU, England.
Tel: (00 44) **0116 236 4325**
Fax: (00 44) **0116 234 0205**

Gunslinger Clint Halloran rides into Plainsville to help his pal Jeff Deacon, hoping to end his friend's troubles. But Deacon is on the point of being lynched, so he fires a shot. Now Halloran has a fight on his hands, a situation complicated by the crooked deputy sheriff, Dan Ramsey, who has his own agenda. Halloran, refusing to give up the fight, vows to keep his gun by his side — right until the final shot is fired.